THE WAR KING

JEANA E. MANN

Ishkadiddle Publishing, LLC

PROLOGUE

ROMAN

The battery on my phone died a few minutes after my phone call to Rourke. I shoved it into the breast pocket of my jacket and rested my head in my hands. *Think, Roman, think.* No one had read my Miranda rights or charged me with a crime. They'd done nothing but ask me the same question over and over.

The door creaked open. Two burly men dressed in identical black trench coats followed the man with flat gray eyes. As I watched, the men stripped out of their coats, folding them before setting them aside. Next, they rolled up their shirtsleeves to reveal thick, muscular forearms covered in sinew and veins. My guts began to churn. This couldn't be good.

"Now, we're going to start again, Roman." Mr. Gray Eyes pulled up a chair in front of me and sat down. "You had seven shipments of arms destined for Saudi Arabia. Only one of those shipments made it. Where are the other six?"

"I have no idea what you're talking about," I said. Of

course, I knew where the guns had gone. The first three shipments had been diverted to Kitzeh, my home country, and the fourth to neighboring Androvia. The rest sat in the basement beneath a donut shop in a small central Indiana town.

"Wrong answer, Roman."

"I can't give you answers that I don't have."

"Let's cut the bullshit." He stood and shook his head. "You received payment in full for a product you didn't deliver. That's not good business. What are we going to do about this?"

"I don't know. Call the Better Business Bureau," I suggested.

With ominous calculation, he cracked each of the knuckles in his right hand, then the left. "You need to get in line, Mr. Menshikov. No one wants to cause a scene. Just do your job, and the threats will end."

"I'm confused. Did you bring me here to charge me with a crime? If so, you need to get on with it."

Hours later, they shoved me into the back of a van. My head cracked against the floor. Darkness swallowed me. I woke up on the hard, wet pavement in an alley behind a Chinese restaurant. My lower lip throbbed from a right hook, but the swelling had stopped. Their other kicks and punches had landed in my midsection. My body ached in previously unknown places. I managed to hobble inside the restaurant and called Spitz.

"You smell like a dead rat," Spitz said, blinking at the aroma wafting from my soiled clothes. "You're gonna stink up my car."

"I'll buy you a new one."

"You need a doctor? Stitches? Anything broken?" His shrewd gaze traveled over my ripped trousers, blood-spattered dress shirt, and fat lip.

"No, I'm good." Thankfully, I'd managed to protect my

healing gunshot wound from their abuse. "I could use a hot shower though." *And Rourke*—I needed her more now than ever. The thought of her sassy mouth and bright smile carried me through the worst of the beating.

He sat behind the wheel and contemplated the trash bins, scattered garbage cans, and a stray tabby cat. "You sure picked a dangerous business. With all your money, you could be sitting on a beach in Fiji, sipping cocktails, and working on your tan."

"I know." This arms project had started to finance Kitzeh's freedom but had quickly grown into a billion-dollar empire. I was in way too far and way too deep to quit, and I'd dragged Rourke into the depths of hell with me.

CHAPTER 1
ROURKE

oman's phone call left me cold and unsettled. *You're going to hear things about me that may or may not be true. I want you to know that I always did what I thought was right.* What had he meant? The man I'd married had no regard for rumors and gossip. But now, I had to wonder if our entire relationship had been an ingenious production of smoke and mirrors. Roman had many layers; lover, father, and shrewd businessman, to name a few. The air of intrigue surrounding him was part of his charm. At least, it had been, until someone had assassinated Ivan, his best friend and mentor.

Times up, Roman. The unfamiliar voice at the end of Roman's call repeated in my dreams. What did that mean? Was he injured? Did he need my help? Frustration tightened the muscles in my forehead and shoulders. Even if he needed my help, I had no idea where he was or who he was with. My feelings bounced from anger to anguish and back again.

After a sleepless night, I texted Spitz, expecting answers, and received nothing. No return phone call. No voice mails. His complete silence frightened me more than any truths he might have revealed. Lance offered little comfort; he knew less than I did.

To distract my mind, I spent the day in Roman's study, reorganizing his files, rummaging for clues to his whereabouts. When I logged into his computer, the screen remained blank and unyielding. His password no longer worked. Desperate for information, I waited for the work day to end then slipped into his downtown office. After a futile search of his desk and files, I climbed into the back of the limo, eager to return home. I drew the edges of my coat tighter as the car took the wrong exit off the freeway. My heart lurched at the unexpected change of direction.

I lowered the partition to question the driver. "Where are we going?" Lance had taken the night off for personal business, leaving me in the hands of an unfamiliar driver.

"I was instructed to take you to the Devil's Playground, Mrs. Menshikov." His unsmiling gaze met mine in the rearview mirror.

"Whose orders?" My pulse escalated. Relief flooded through me. At least Roman was okay.

"Mr. Menshikov, ma'am."

"I want to go home." Although I needed answers, Roman's highhandedness spurred my rebellious nature. Now that I knew he wasn't in trouble, anger crept in to replace the relief.

"I'm sorry, ma'am. I have my orders."

"Turn the car around," I snapped.

"No disrespect, Mrs. Menshikov, but I don't work for you." With an apologetic nod, he raised the partition.

Outside the car, the city lights streaked through the night. I shoved back in the seat, seething with fury, knowing that further protests would go unheeded. I'd been summoned to the court of the exiled prince, and there was nothing I could do about it. With every passing mile, my anxiety climbed to new heights.

When the car stopped at the nondescript back door of the Devil's Playground NYC, a thin sheen of perspiration chilled my skin. The last time I'd been here, I'd been filled with nervousness for different, more pleasant reasons. Reluctantly, I climbed out of the limo and rang the buzzer. Achilles opened the door immediately. His expression face yielded nothing.

"Good evening. May I take your wrap?" Under his watchful gaze, I slipped out of my light jacket and handed it to him. He draped it over his arm then pulled a red blindfold from his pocket. "You'll need to put this on."

"Why?" I stared at the blindfold, unable to fathom the rules of this newest game, a game I wasn't sure I wanted to play.

"I have no idea, madam."

"I know. I know." I cut him off mid-sentence. "My husband's orders."

"Yes, madam." He clasped his hands in front of him and waited.

"Fine." I kept my tone even and placed the blindfold over my eyes. My fight was with Roman, not Achilles, and it would be unfair to take my wrath out on his employee. The silk slipped through my trembling fingers, but I finally managed to tie the knot. Robbed of my sight, the rest of my senses leaped into action. The scents of floor polish and Achilles's aftershave jumped to the forefront. The faint notes of classical music hovered in the air, too soft to be identified.

"Excellent. If you'll allow me to take your hand, I'll guide you to your husband."

I jumped at his cool touch on my wrist. Taking my hand, he curled my fingers into the crook of his elbow.

Our footsteps echoed on the hard floor—his certain and

mine hesitant. We passed through several corridors, winding our way into the unknown. When he opened the next door, loud techno music pulsed through the walls, making conversation impossible. My heart clanged against my ribs, knowing that each stride brought me closer to Roman. Equal measures of anticipation and anxiety warred inside me.

After a lengthy journey, Achilles halted. I strained for clues: the rustle of clothing, the click of a key in a lock, the quiet creak of hinges. He led me into what I presumed was one of the playrooms. "Wait here, madam," he said. I reached for the blindfold, but he closed a hand over mine. "Don't remove the blindfold."

"Wait." I reached in front of me, finding nothing but empty air. "Achilles, where are you going?" Standing alone, unable to see, my panic escalated. His footsteps faded to the rear. The door creaked shut, and the lock clicked.

"Don't be afraid." Roman's deep voice rumbled at my side.

"I'm not afraid. I'm furious." Even while I protested, my chest heaved with excitement. The scent of his cologne—peppery, familiar, and sweet—tickled my nose. "Why am I blindfolded?"

"Because it pleases me." The command in his voice weakened my knees. This was the Roman I loved, the man who ruled my heart and my body without mercy.

"I don't appreciate being kidnapped." In the absence of sight, my senses sharpened. Light footsteps circled me. I turned, trying to follow his path.

"And yet, here you are."

"I hardly had a choice. I asked to be taken home. Your driver refused."

"You always have a choice, Cinderella." His breath brushed my right ear. I gasped at the delicious spread of goosebumps down the back of my neck.

"If you wanted to talk to me, you could have called on the phone like a normal person."

His voice moved to my left. I whipped my head to follow his movements. "I could have, but then again, we both know I'm not a normal person, right? I'm arrogant and dirty and perverted." The backs of his fingers skimmed up my bare forearm. I shivered. "This seemed like a lot more fun."

"Don't play with me." An ache unfurled in the pit of my belly. Although I complained, I wanted him to do just that. *Take me. Fuck me. Make me whole again.*

"I want you back." The stubble of his chin scraped along my jaw. I whimpered, knowing his lips hovered mere inches away. "You belong to me. I've barely touched you, yet your nipples are poking through your dress, taunting me." To prove his point, he pinched one of them, making me hiss at the sting of pleasure. "Your rejection makes me crazy."

"Your call this morning—what was that about? I've been out of mind with worry. Was it another one of your mind games?"

"A bad move on my part. I'm sorry for putting you through that." The heat of his body warmed my backside. "I let circumstances get the better of me, and I apologize. It won't happen again." His soft lips nibbled along the bend of my jaw. The muscles below my waist clenched in response. "But I needed to hear your voice, to touch you, and the situation seemed...desperate."

"Where were you? Give me answers." This was just like him, to play with my head and tug at my heartstrings. As my fury grew, so did my lust for him. They were irrevocably entwined, each feeding the other.

"You'll get them, but not tonight." The tip of his nose traced the curve of my ear. Against my will, my body leaned into him, drawn by a force more powerful than gravity. "Tonight isn't about excuses or explanations. I brought you here to remind you of how we began." A slight tug preceded the growl of the zipper down my back. Fresh air wafted over the skin laid bare as my dress parted. His fingertips smoothed along the curve of my spine.

"Is anyone watching us?" The playrooms had been designed with walls of mirrored glass. The voyeuristic members of the club could observe and listen at the discretion of the occupants. The thought added to the slickness gathering between my thighs.

"Maybe." His teeth nipped the bend of my shoulder. I whimpered, shifting my weight from one foot to the next, seeking to ease the ache of desire growing inside me. "Would you like that, my dirty princess?"

"Yes." I bit my lower lip to keep from whimpering. "I mean, no."

"Maybe there's a whole gallery of people watching me strip your gorgeous body."

"I'm not going to have sex with you," I said, in a final attempt to gain control of the situation.

"I can respect that. I wouldn't expect any other answer from you, considering my recent bad behavior." The loss of his body heat signaled his retreat. The removal of his lips from my skin filled me with disappointment and confusion.

"Where are you going?" Somehow, he'd turned the tables. Part of me wanted to scream at him, while the rest of me wanted him to fuck me senseless. How could I be so angry and so in love at the same time? The Victorian romance novels in my library had never mentioned this kind of conflict.

"I'm right here, but I'll go if you want."

"Not—not yet." I held the front of my dress to my breasts with one arm.

"Do you want more?"

"Yes." I whispered the word, ashamed of my desperation for his touch.

"Drop your dress." The sharp command sent adrenalin rushing through my veins. I let the knee-length linen puddle at my feet. Gooseflesh pebbled my arms and legs. The roughness of his palms skated over my breasts, cupping them, then caught the edges of my panties and dragged them down my legs. "Step out."

I lifted my feet, letting him dispose of the thin lace.

His footsteps circled me again. "Very nice."

"I'm glad you approve." I liked knowing he desired my body with its lumps and bumps and cellulite. I exhaled to calm my soaring heart rate. Where was he taking us? This game might have been unexpected, but I opened my mind to the possibilities. A little playtime might bring us back to common ground.

His hands bracketed my hips, his lips close to my ear. "Lift your arms. There are two ropes above your head. I want you to wrap them around your wrists and hold on."

"What are you going to do to me?" My voice came out raspy and breathless. I trembled with excitement.

"Trust me." He guided my hands to the soft braided ropes. The fabric of his shirt whispered across my back, my left arm, and finally my breasts as he came to stand in front of me.

I leaned into him. His shirt buttons bit into my breasts, and the hardness between his legs nudged my belly. "Why are you still dressed?"

"Until tonight, I've been holding back with you, but not anymore. It's become apparent to me that life is fleeting. You want to know the real me—well, this is just a small part of who I am." His arms wrapped around my waist and crushed me to him. I soaked up his strong embrace. "I can take you places you've never been before, Rourke, if you can accept my world."

I didn't have time to contemplate the double-edged meaning of his words. He kissed a burning trail down the column of my neck, pausing to suck each of my nipples, then continuing down my belly. The heat of his breath tickled against my flesh. His lips dragged down to my hips, his hair sweeping over my pelvis.

"Don't let go of the ropes. I'd tie you up, but I don't think you're ready for that quite yet." His words vibrated against the insides of my thighs. "Put your leg over my shoulder." With a hand behind my knee, he steadied me, opening me to him. His next kiss landed directly on my sex. I threw my head back and moaned.

God, I'd missed his mouth. It worshipped me, punctuated by tiny flicks of his tongue against my clit. I gripped the ropes tighter. My fingers ached. He pulled me to him, his hands on my bottom. The tip of his nose nudged my folds. With his face between my legs, he sucked and nipped. One of his fingers thrust inside me. I cried out, not caring who heard or was watching.

"Yes. Please. Yes." I struggled to keep my balance while he dragged me to the edge of oblivion. In my head, I pictured him on his knees in his black trousers and crisp white dress shirt, clinging to my bottom, wringing every ounce of pleasure from my naked body. My loud cries echoed through the room. As warning tremors shook my legs, I thrust my pelvis forward, trying to ride his mouth, desperate for release.

My words spurred his efforts. He thrust two more fingers inside me, curling them upward to hit my most secret place, and I lost control. My walls contracted. I released the ropes and dug my fingers into his hair, rocking against his face, crazy with need. My clutching hands stirred the scent of his shampoo. Waves of pleasure raced through my center, radiating out to the tips of my fingers and toes.

"That's my girl. Give me everything. I want all of you," he

said, timing the pace of his fingers to the rhythm of my inner contractions. I clenched around him, riding the high of the most unbelievable orgasm I'd ever had.

This was what I needed. Him. His mouth. His fingers. His touch. I'd never been so torn and so complete in my entire life. Roman Menshikov ruled my world, and I was a fool for doubting it.

CHAPTER 2
ROMAN

This playroom had been specifically designed to suit my basest desires. Removable wood panels covered soundproof concrete walls, ready to be changed out to suit my moods. A wall of mirrors reflected Rourke's naked body and hid the observation room behind it. Her legs trembled from her orgasm. One of them remained wrapped around my shoulders. She had said she didn't know me, and maybe she didn't. Until this morning, I'd been unable to show my darkness to her. If I wanted to keep her, I'd have to reveal the parts I'd kept hidden. It was a gamble that scared the living shit out of me.

"I need to sit down." Her voice wavered. She was still clutching my hair.

I slid my hands up the backs of her legs and stood, pulling her to me. God, she felt amazing, all boneless and sated from my mouth on her pussy. I squeezed her tighter, making her whimper. "Did you enjoy that, baby?"

"Yes, but I need to see you." She reached for her blindfold.

"No." I grabbed her hands. "You can't." Over her shoulder,

I gazed at my reflection in the mirrors. My battered face stared back at me. "Not like this."

"Why? What's wrong? Did something happen?" Her voice raised in alarm. At least she still cared. She tried to touch my face.

I caught her wrist and pulled it away. "I said no, Cinderella."

"You say you want me to know the real you and then you hide things from me. It's not fair."

"Life isn't fair." I disentangled myself from her and backed away a few steps. Her breasts heaved with her rapid breathing. "You know that."

"It doesn't mean I have to like it." She wobbled on her high heels before regaining her balance. "Tell me."

I stroked a hand along the side of her face, her skin silky beneath my touch. "Some bad men tried to scare me into submission. Unfortunately for them, I don't scare easily." How could I explain when I didn't understand, either? The less she knew, the better for both of us.

"Don't do this." She yanked away her blindfold, but I'd already slipped through the secret door into the adjoining observation room.

Behind the one-way glass, I watched her face redden with frustration. She spun in a circle, scanning the room, unfazed by her nakedness. She'd come a long way from the modest girl I'd met last year.

"Where are you?" Her gaze fell on the mirror in front of me. She stalked over to the glass and stared directly into my eyes. I took a step back before remembering that she couldn't see me, she was merely guessing at my location. "If you're trying to make things better, this isn't helping. You're just pissing me off." Her last sentence ended in a shout.

I stared into her delicate face, separated from mine by a few inches and a thin sheet of glass, admiring the fire in her eyes. This was the woman I'd married, a hellcat, the only person besides Ivan to call out my bullshit. She banged a hand against the mirror, pivoted, and began gathering her clothes from the floor.

I'd brought her here because I couldn't stand the separation, sleeping alone, wondering if she was okay. I needed her. She'd gotten under my skin. She was a part of me now, the *best* part of me. I pressed the intercom speaker, but it was too late. Fully dressed, she plunged out of the playroom. The door slammed shut behind her.

Someone knocked on the door. I quickly hit the control panel, shimmering the glass from clear to mirrored, and said, "Come in."

Spitz entered the room, his eyebrows lifting to the edge of his hairline. "I think I just passed your wife. She broke a lamp on her way out. Trouble in paradise?"

I ignored his question. "Have you found out who did this to me?"

"I spoke with my contacts at the agency. No one knows anything about this." He shrugged. "My gut tells me this is an independent—someone gone rogue, abusing their power to try and manipulate you." He scratched his chin. Neither of us had shaved in a few days. Strands of gray peppered the stubble on his cheeks. "I think you need to leave the Four Seasons. It would be even better if you moved back to your penthouse. Somewhere we can control."

I ignored his request, unwilling to delve into the wreckage of my marriage. "Put a tail on my wife. Double her security. Don't let her out of your sight."

Spitz stared at me, his eyelids narrowing. "Personally, boss, I think you need to reevaluate your commitment to this woman."

A fury unlike anything I'd ever felt welled up inside me. I grabbed him by the neck and pinned him to the wall. "You're out of line. Give me one good reason why I shouldn't fire your ass right now." He had more than enough self-defense skills to kill me with his bare hands. To his credit, he remained calm and unblinking.

"Someone inside your circle is giving out confidential information. Who better than your wife? I mean, what do you know about her, really?" He lifted both hands in the air, palms facing outward. "I'd be remiss if I didn't mention the possibility."

I let go of his throat and backed away, my hands shaking. "Spoken like a man who's been divorced a half-dozen times."

"You mean spoken like a man who's been fucked over by women more than his fair share." He straightened his collar, calm and unruffled.

"My wife isn't like that."

"All women are like that." We stared at each other for an uncomfortable minute.

"If we're going to continue this business partnership, you need to understand that my wife and daughter are the most important parts of my life. I won't tolerate your disrespect toward either one of them."

He paced the length of the room before coming to a stop at in front of me. "I know I'm on shaky ground here, but you need to keep your distance from her. Someone might follow her to you."

"I'll be careful." Asking me to stay away from Rourke was like demanding me to stop breathing. I'd already been apart from her for an eternity, and I was done sleeping alone.

CHAPTER 3
ROURKE

The floor-to-ceiling windows of my penthouse bedroom offered the best view in all of New York City, but the Manhattan morning skyline did nothing for the ache in my chest or the emptiness in my heart. Roman's stunt at the Devil's Playground NYC yesterday had left me with more questions than answers. I pressed two fingers to my lips, savoring the burn of his kisses, and prayed for a resolution to our problems.

"Ladies, concentrate." Christian, my friend and personal stylist, clapped his hands, and called order to the chaos in the room. "Rourke, are you listening to me?"

"Yes. Sorry." I'd completely forgotten about Everly's fundraiser until Christian had shown up this morning with an entourage and a cartful of formal ensembles. He spread an array of designer ball gowns across the room. The piles of silk looked like resting butterflies on the enormous king-size bed. He fussed and fluffed and tugged at the blue taffeta Vera Wang I was wearing until I heaved an enormous sigh.

The last place I wanted to be was in a roomful of strangers discussing something as trivial as haute couture, not with the space between my legs aching and the Playground fresh in my memories. Despite Roman's promises that everything would be fine, uneasiness churned in my stomach. Memories of the way he'd brought me to climax flooded my cheeks with heat. Although I was furious at his highhandedness, I secretly hoped he'd kidnap me again. The whole situation had whipped my emotions into a frenzy.

Christian tugged at the lapels of his blue silk shirt and snapped his fingers at one of the assistants. "She hates it. Bring me the yellow Dior."

"I don't hate it. I was thinking of something else." I smoothed my hands down the soft fabric and stared at my reflection in the full-length mirror. It was the fifth gown I'd tried on. Did Roman like yellow? Then I remembered. He wasn't going to the ball with me. I'd be flying solo to this event. I swallowed down the thickness in my throat.

"Don't lie. It's written all over that pretty face of yours. Never fear. Christian has brought the answer to your prayers." He clapped his hands, prompting the assistants to unzip my gown and strip me to my underwear. At first, I'd been embarrassed to stand in front of virtual strangers in my bra and panties, but after the second fitting, I'd become used to it. Christian had assured me that none of my girl parts excited him, and his female assistants were too frightened of him to do more than follow his barked orders.

"How much does a gown like this cost, anyway?" I tried to search for a price tag, but he smacked my hand away.

"Don't worry about the money. Your fine-ass husband said to spare no expense and to give you anything you want." He ducked to admire his reflection in the mirror and to rearrange the spikes of his trendy haircut.

"He told you that? Directly? When?"

"Of course he did, from the very first day. He was adamant. You're the cherry on his sundae, the sugar in his coffee, the cream cheese on his bagel, the——" At the sight of my raised eyebrows, he stopped and took a new direction. "If you must know, this one is forty thousand."

"Are you kidding me?"

"I don't kid about money or clothing. You know this."

One of the housemaids walked in with a tray of fresh fruit, chicken salad, and lemon water. She kept her eyes averted from my nakedness. "Is there anything else, Mrs. Menshikov?"

"No, thank you. Unless you and the girls want something?" I turned to Christian, who was holding the Dior dress up to the light and frowning.

"No. We're not your guests. We work for you. You wouldn't offer lunch to the gardener, would you?"

"I don't know." As a former personal assistant to Everly and then Roman, I still hadn't wrapped my head around the transition from struggling employee to fabulously wealthy socialite. I knew firsthand how it felt to be in service to someone else. In fact, overcome by the solitude of the penthouse, I'd been eating supper in the kitchen with the cook. Roman would've had a fit had he known. But Roman wasn't here. I blinked away the sting of tears. "Maybe. If he was hungry. Gardeners need to eat, too."

My answer made Christian's eyes bulge. "Listen up. You're the queen bee of Manhattan. The sooner you start acting like it, the better. What's wrong with you?"

Everything. The word scrolled through my thoughts on a marquis, replaying until I wanted to scream. An overwhelming urge to bolt twitched through my toes. I wanted to run home to Aunt May and the comfort of our two-bedroom bungalow, to eat at a fast food chain without an entourage of bodyguards, and take walks in Central Park alone, but I couldn't. Aunt May was dead, her house sold, and I was the wife of the most powerful man in New York City, if not the world.

"No. No. No. What are you doing? Get out of here." He yanked a Hermes scarf out of the hands of a young woman and shouted into the vastness of the bedroom, scattering all of the assistants into the hallway like frightened mice. "I swear, it's impossible to get good help these days." The silk of the next gown rustled as he dropped it over my head and tugged it into place. "What about this one?"

"I like it. What about you? Do you like it?" In truth, I didn't give two shits about the dress. Where the hell was Roman, and why all the mystery? I glanced at my phone resting on the dresser, like it might offer an answer. After last night's tryst, I'd hoped he would call. My phone remained silent, and I was too proud to reach out to him first.

"Rourke. Snap out of it. It's not about what I want; it's about you. What do you want?"

"I don't know." I stepped down from the stool and sat on the edge of the bed. "You decide."

He placed both hands on his hips and shook his head. "You know what your problem is? You've spent so much time in the shadows of Everly and Prince Hottie that you've forgotten who Rourke is. You're acting like you're still someone else's personal assistant when you're the one with all the power. Don't you understand? With one snap of your fingers, you can *have* anything—*do* anything—you want in this world."

"If only it was that simple." I sighed.

"Where's that fierce girl I met five years ago? Bring her out. I miss her." He flapped his hands, motioning for me to stand up. "Now get your ass off that bed. You're disrespecting the Dior."

"Maybe I should cancel tomorrow night." The thought of walking alone into a ballroom brimming with the country's wealthiest citizens made my stomach flip. I'd accepted the invitation months earlier, before Ivan's death and my disagreement with Roman. It seemed like a lifetime ago. Although Roman and I hadn't publicly announced our separation, speculation and lies had infiltrated social media. There were bound to be questioning stares and whispers. I shifted from one foot to the other, contemplating and getting nowhere.

"Oh, no. You're going if I have to drive you myself. I don't have a license or a car, so it might get a little scary." He glared. After a moment, his expression softened, and his voice turned sticky sweet. "Come on, baby girl. You don't want to disappoint Everly, do you? This is her biggest event of the year. How's she going to feel if her best friend stands her up?"

"Fine. I get your point." This was the longest Everly and I had ever gone without speaking to each other. I couldn't give her another reason to be disappointed in me. On the other hand, maybe she didn't want me at the event. Pain pricked my chest. I'd managed to alienate everyone in my life. I had a luxurious penthouse, an indecent amount of money, and no one to share it with.

"Goodness, girl. Those bags under your eyes look like you're going on a grand tour of Europe. Can I get some concealer in here? Where is everyone?" He turned in a circle, hands extended, shouting into the empty room. "And what's going on around your middle? You've got a pooch." His nimble fingers adjusted the sash around my waist to hide the extra pounds I'd put on over the past month. Food had become a source of solace. "I'll have to let this out a little."

"Okay." I yawned.

"Mrs. Menshikov, excuse me." A second housemaid stood on the threshold of the bedroom, overwhelmed by Christian's glare. "Mr. Menshikov's new personal assistant has arrived.

He's getting his things moved into the apartment downstairs. I thought you would want to know."

"Yes, thanks. I appreciate the head's up." A flicker of annoyance burned in my belly. I stared at the new dress in the mirror and struggled to control my temper. Roman had fired me as his personal assistant, claiming it was an unsuitable occupation for his wife. Now that he'd hired someone else, the finality stung. I clenched my fingers at my sides. My old life had slipped away, and I was powerless to stop it.

The maid hovered. Her occasional glances at Christian suggested she harbored a healthy fear of him.

"Is there something else?" I asked.

"Um, Mr. Spitz has asked to see you. He's waiting in the foyer."

"Send him up." I shifted uneasily against the scratchy inner seams of the gown. For forty thousand dollars, the dress should have a gold lining. At the same time, an unwelcome shiver ran up my spine. Was Spitz bearing bad news? Or was Roman summoning me again?

"To your bedroom? Are you sure?" The maid shook her head. "Mr. Menshikov never allows guests in his bedroom—aside from you, of course."

I frowned. Had she just referred to me as a guest? "It's *my* bedroom, Janet, and you're right. Of course. What was I thinking?" Lack of sleep was twisting my common sense. A deep breath steadied my nerves. "Tell him I'll be down in a minute. No, wait, I'll go myself." I hopped off the stool. On bare feet, I trotted down the hall and descended the sweeping staircase. The silk gown rustled with each step.

Christian followed on my heels, muttering. "Forty thousand dollars, Rourke."

"I'm good for it," I replied.

Spitz stood at the bottom of the stairs. His eyes widened at the sight of the expensive silk dress, Christian, and my bare feet. The air in the room chilled. He bowed his salt-and-pepper head, shoulders erect. He ran a finger along the inside of the collar of his black dress shirt, like he'd rather be anywhere else.

"What's wrong? Is Roman okay?"

"He's fine, ma'am. I'm here to inform you that I've doubled your security, and I'd like to request that you keep your social activities to a minimum while we work through the situation." His gaze flitted to the handful of assistants who'd followed me and Christian downstairs.

"I'm going to a charity ball tomorrow night. Will that be a problem?"

"Lance has informed me. We've made arrangements to keep you safe." The chill in his tone sent a shiver down my back.

"Should we go to Roman's study to discuss this?"

He lifted a hand. "No need. You seem busy. I'm done."

"Wait." I followed him toward the door. "Is that it?"

"Well, now that you mention it..." The blunt tips of his fingers scratched over his jaw. "There is something bothering me. If you cared about your husband's safety, he'd be living here and not in some hotel."

"He's at the Four Seasons. It's not like he's in a tent underneath a bridge." Having seen the opulence of the hotel penthouse a few times before, his argument held little weight. I rolled my eyes.

"And here you are, the suffering wife, prancing around his Manhattan penthouse in fancy dresses with your entourage."

His words stung. I reeled back like I'd been struck. "What's that supposed to mean?" My temper flared. "Did he say something to you?"

"No, just my opinion." The elevator beeped, and the doors opened. He nodded, his gaze chilly. "You have a good day, Mrs. Menshikov." With a crisp pivot, he strode into the waiting car, leaving me open-mouthed beneath the grand chandelier.

The doors closed. His insult burned, hot and intrusive. I clenched my fists, wanting to run after him and demand an apology. I stabbed at the elevator button, but it was a long way to the bottom. By the time the car returned, my temper had cooled. Screw Spitz. I had bigger issues to worry about right now. Although I wanted to run to Roman, I couldn't make myself go. He was a warlord, and the thought turned my stomach. How many innocent people had died from his actions? I'd never touched a gun and never would. If I went to him, I'd be condoning his actions, and I just couldn't. Not yet. Maybe not ever.

Let it go, Rourke. I exhaled and turned to leave but barreled into a slender young man with round glasses.

"Sorry. So sorry," he said, pushing his glasses back up his nose.

"Who are you?" His short, curly hair and unsmiling face were unfamiliar. I glanced around for a staff member, panicked to see a stranger in my home. For once, I was alone. They'd probably evacuated to the back of the penthouse to avoid Christian.

"I'm Percy, Mr. Menshikov's new assistant. And you're Mrs. Menshikov?" He extended a tentative hand.

"Um, yes." The tension eased from my shoulders. Worried brown eyes studied mine. At second glance, he seemed much younger—maybe early twenties. "Nice to meet you, Percy. I hope you're getting settled in okay?"

"I am. Thank you." He rolled his lips together and glanced from side to side. "I'll be ready to start tomorrow. Mr. Menshikov said you'd be training me."

"Did he?" I held back a scathing tirade of profanity. Roman felt I wasn't capable of being his personal assistant, but he wanted me to train my replacement. Fat chance. "Well, he was mistaken." Then my conscience got the better of me. I knew how intimidating Roman could be and how unsettling the first day of any job felt. "I've got a lot on my plate right now, but I'll make sure you have someone show you the ropes."

"Thank you. I appreciate it."

"You're welcome. Please let Janet know if you need anything." I swept the long dress away from my feet and trotted up the staircase. Even though Roman had left, he still ordered me around like an employee, and it had to stop. If he wanted a high society wife, he was going to get one. However, it would be on my terms. Not his.

CHAPTER 4
ROURKE

The next evening, I walked into The Grand Ballroom of The Plaza Hotel, feeling like a new kid on the first day of school. After a fortifying breath, I lifted my chin and did my best not to trip over the long hem of the yellow Dior. The last time I'd been here, I'd been Everly's employee, not a guest. Dozens of watchful eyes tracked my progress as I crossed the glossy floor. Beneath the enormous crystal chandeliers, Manhattan's finest dignitaries chatted, laughed, and plotted world domination. I scanned the sea of black tuxedos and colorful gowns for anyone I might know but came up empty until the familiar gazes of Everly's parents turned in my direction.

"Rourke, darling, how wonderful to see you." Judy McElroy greeted me with air kisses on each cheek.

"Yes, it's been too long. How are you?" Don McElroy's warm hands enveloped mine and squeezed.

"I'm good. Thanks. It's wonderful to see you, too." Affection swelled inside me as I greeted two of my dearest friends. Although they would never replace Mom and Dad, they had endeavored to fill the gaps left by their passing and never failed to include me in their family gatherings. I owed them more than I could ever hope to repay.

"Goodness, you're pale. Do you need to sit down?" She caressed my cheek. Lines of worry crinkled around her eyes. The scent of her Chanel perfume took me back to the days of playing dress-up with Everly and raiding her mother's cosmetic drawer.

"I'm fine. Just a little overwhelmed by all the grandeur." I smiled to cover up my uncertainties. Smiling could hide a multitude of sins, even for a sinner like me.

"Everly will be delighted to see you. She thought you might not show. Where did she go?" Mr. McElroy draped a comforting arm around my shoulders as he searched the crowd for his daughter.

"I'm sure she's busy. I don't want to bother her while she's working." I had no idea what kind of greeting to expect from her and didn't have the strength for another argument. Her feelings for Nicky ran deeper than I'd realized. I vowed to keep my opinions about her love life to myself.

A passing waiter offered champagne from a gleaming gold tray. I took one of the flutes and tossed back the entire glass. A little bubbly might calm my nerves. On the other hand, the last thing I wanted to do was become tipsy in front of Roman's colleagues and Everly's parents.

"I see Maxwell Seaforth over there." Mr. McElroy squeezed me before taking his wife's hand. "Rourke, please excuse us. We need to speak with him before he slips out of here."

"Oh, dear, I'm so sorry to leave you alone. Will you be okay?" I nodded, and Mrs. McElroy smiled. "Of course you will. You must come for dinner tomorrow night."

"I'd love that. Thank you." Spending time with the McElroys sounded a lot better than wallowing in misery at home, stuffing my face with junk food, and binging Netflix.

They disappeared into the crowd, leaving me alone. I wanted to melt into one of the quiet corners and hide. Instead, I wandered through the crowd and tried to ignore the whispers and stares.

"Isn't that Roman's new wife?"

"Can you believe he married his personal assistant?"

"I thought she'd be thinner."

"I heard they're already separated."

Why, why, why had I come tonight? My insecurities flared to maximum strength. I'd never been comfortable in the spotlight. That had always been Everly's forte. She knew how to work the room, to put people at ease, and looked like a queen while doing it. I smoothed the front of my gown, wondering if the Dior had been a mistake. The yellow silk gleamed like a beacon in the sea of black, beige, and silver. Maybe I should have chosen something less noticeable.

"Rourke? You came." Everly glided toward me, a vision of loveliness in pale blue organza, and I relaxed. The tight mermaid dress accentuated her tiny waist and D-cup boobs. Her flowing red hair gleamed beneath the chandeliers. No one would notice me with her around.

"I promised, didn't I?" I extended a hand but froze when a pair of dark eyes caught mine from across the room.

Roman stood under one of the arches near the orchestra, surrounded by a handful of men. My heart skipped a beat at the sight of his broad shoulders beneath a black tuxedo jacket. His gaze locked onto mine. Without a second glance at his companions, he strode across the floor, ignoring hopeful greetings from other guests, making a direct path toward me. Goodness, had he always been so charismatic, so gorgeous?

I placed a hand on my diaphragm, feeling like all the oxygen had been sucked from the room.

"—and we both know how that went." Everly had been speaking to me, and I hadn't heard a word.

"Um, sorry?" I cleared my throat and tried to focus on her face instead of Roman's intense stare. With each of his approaching steps, my blood pressure spiked higher and higher until black spots swam in front of my eyes. What was he doing here? He hated these types of affairs, finding them pretentious and unbearable.

"I said, I'm still angry at your for judging my relationship with Nicky, and you're not forgiven, but I'm glad you're here." She touched my elbow, drawing my attention back to her. "Now isn't the time to discuss it, though. We can talk later. In the meantime, what do you think of my event?"

"It looks lovely. You did an amazing job, as always." For the first time, I met her gaze and flinched at the mixture of hurt and coolness in the depths of her eyes. A thin veneer of politeness masked her features; a look reserved for strangers and business associates. The lump in my throat grew larger. In the meantime, Roman was only a few paces away and drawing nearer with every heartbeat.

"I've had nothing but problems," she said, shaking her head. "You always made sure things ran smoothly. My new girl is good, but she doesn't have your experience."

"I'm sure she'll catch up." Someone stepped in front of Roman, blocking his progress. My palms began to sweat.

"The florist was late, and the caterer made the wrong hors d'oeuvres." Her expression brightened. "Hey, I don't suppose I could bribe you to check with the chef and make sure everything is back on track?" She lifted her eyebrows hopefully. "You'd be doing me a huge favor."

"Well..." I glanced at Roman. The predatory gleam of his dark eyes dissolved the strength in my knees. I needed to escape—fast. "Okay sure."

"Thanks. You're a doll." She squeezed my hand and turned to greet a new guest.

My heart pounded. The last thing I needed tonight was an altercation with my husband in front of all these strangers. By the purpose in his stride, he had plenty to say. If he asked to come home with me, I'd cave to his wishes. Or even worse, I might beg him to return when we still had issues to resolve.

I pushed through the swinging doors into the kitchen and leaned against the wall to steady my nerves. The aromas of spices and garlic, something I usually found appealing, turned my stomach. The chef cast a questioning glare at me. I smiled. "Ms. McElroy sent me to check on your progress. Are we back on track?" Years of experience kicked in. I fell back into my role of personal assistant with ease, finding comfort in its familiarity. "Do you need anything?"

"Yes, we're good, but two of our waiters quit—like, five minutes ago. Those trays are ready to go out." He nodded toward several trays of mouthwatering appetizers.

"I'll take them." Without a moment's hesitation, I hoisted one of the trays into the air, pushed through the swinging doors, and came face-to-face with my husband. My stomach churned at the sight of the split in his lip. A cut on his chin held two stitches. Green and purple tinged his left eye. It took all of my self-control to keep from bursting into tears over his mistreatment.

"Whoa." He caught the tray, narrowly avoiding a crash, and placed it on the table in the hallway. "What the fuck is this?"

"Bacon-wrapped dates with almonds, caviar, and that looks like some kind of quiche." My hands trembled. I clasped them behind my back. Damn him for affecting me this way.

"I know what they are. I meant, why are you carrying a serving tray?" In the narrow hallway, he seemed taller and larger. Oh God, he was handsomer than ever. The injuries to his face gave him a dangerous demeanor. His delectable lips thinned into a straight line of displeasure. I summoned the willpower to keep from kissing him.

"Everly needed help." *Don't look into his eyes.* One glance into his beautiful blue irises, and I'd be lost.

"You don't work for Everly anymore."

"Well, apparently, I don't work for you either. I met your new assistant today." The recollection spurred my temper.

"Are you ever going to get over that?" He groaned but curbed his wrath when a waiter entered the corridor with us. He gestured toward the tray, his voice menacing. "You. Take that, and get out."

The poor guy snatched the food and fled in the opposite direction.

"I'll get over it when you stop making decisions without my input." I lifted my chin and glared at him.

"You've got to move past this, Rourke. Are we going to stay stuck in limbo forever?" He stared down his straight nose at me. When I didn't answer, he took a step closer, minimizing the gap between us until the buttons of his tuxedo brushed the tips of my breasts. I could smell his cologne, spicy and sweet, and the sharpness of whisky on his breath.

"What happened to you?" Overwhelmed by concern, I forgot to be angry. Using a tentative fingertip, I touched his lip.

"I'm fine. Nothing for you to worry about." The line of his jaw became harder and squarer. Black stubble peppered his cheeks. On most men, an unshaven face would seem disrespectful in The Plaza, but the rough whiskers gave him a devilish air and made my blood sing, the same stubble that had left a red rash on my inner thighs.

"Aren't you afraid people will ask questions?"

"As far as everyone else is concerned, these bruises are

from an unfortunate round of boxing with my trainer. Not that I give a fuck what anyone thinks." He rested a hand against the wall above my shoulder and leaned closer. I swallowed and tried to calm my rapid pulse. "What's the matter, Rourke? Aren't you happy to see me?" His words, which were usually precise and crisp, blurred together.

With both palms on his chest, I tried to push him away, but his strong arms formed a cage around me. I turned my head away. "You're drunk."

"Of course I'm drunk. I got my ass kicked by two very large, very ugly henchmen, and to top things off, my wife left me." His breath seared my cheek. "I think I deserve to get shit-faced, don't you?"

"I didn't leave you. We're taking a break."

"Semantics. No matter what you call it, we can both agree that we aren't living under the same roof, and things aren't looking good for us."

"After your stunt at the Devil's Playground, how did you expect me to act?" I tried to wriggle away from him, but he stepped closer, trapping me against the wall with his broad chest. "You're making me nervous."

"Good. If you're nervous, it means you care." The tip of his nose dragged along the side of my face until his mouth rested against my temple. "You still love me, right?"

"Not when you're like this," I said, finding my resolve again.

"You might not like me, but I suspect you're turned on." His mouth trailed a hot, wet line down to my collarbone. "I bet if I checked, your panties would be soaked."

In response to his claim, I pressed my legs together against the delicious ache between my thighs. My panties were indeed drenched, but I couldn't help it. Having him this close turned me on and reminded me of the way he'd brought me to ecstasy in the playroom. I twisted my fingers in the lapels of his jacket.

"You know I'm wet for you. Just because we're having problems doesn't mean I don't want you. Sex has never been the issue."

"Then come upstairs with me." His hand found the slit in my gown and walked up the inside of my thigh to the lace-trimmed edge of my panties. I gasped as his index finger slipped beneath the hem and brushed my clit.

"I thought you were at the Four Seasons."

"I was, and now I'm not. I'm staying here."

I fought to keep my head clear while he made tiny circles on my sensitive nub. Echoes of pleasure radiated through my center. Why did he have to be so good at this? Damn him. "I need to go."

"God, you're drenched. I want you, Rourke. If you don't come upstairs with me, I'm going to take you here. Now. Is that what you want?"

He didn't give me time to answer before his mouth covered mine. His tongue ravaged me, searing my taste buds with the burn of whisky. I clung tighter to his jacket, not caring that someone might see us, or that I was still angry with him. He felt familiar and exciting and safe. I drank him in, using all my senses, trembling from the force of my desire.

"Oh. Sorry." From far away, Everly's surprised greeting cut through my fog of sexual frustration. "I'll just go…" Her voice faded as she trotted back toward the direction she'd come from.

"No. Wait. It's okay. I was just coming to find you." I let my hands fall from Roman's jacket and cast my gaze to Everly.

"Right." Roman stepped aside and shoved a hand through his hair. "Sure. Go ahead. Run away again."

I smoothed my palms over the rumpled front of my dress. "Unless you plan to tell me what's going on with you, we have nothing more to say to each other. Call me when you're sober."

He leaned against the wall, both hands in his pockets, brows lowered.

I fled toward Everly and escape. Yes, I was running away from him again, but I didn't know what else to do. Running was easier than facing our problems—problems I didn't know how to fix.

Everly drew me into the ladies' room and began touching up my smudged makeup. "What was that all about? He looked super angry."

"Things are—are difficult." This was the understatement of the year, but I didn't want to go into the details of my shattered marriage in a public toilet. "He saw me carrying a tray of hors d'oeuvres and went ballistic. He said I wasn't your employee, and I needed to stop acting like it."

Everly's gaze softened. "He's right. You're a paying guest. I took advantage of your niceness, and I shouldn't have."

"It was just a tray of food. I'm happy to help out whenever you need it." My frustration began to build again. Clearly, I kept crossing the invisible lines of class distinction. "What's the big deal?"

"You're Mrs. Menshikov." She stared at our reflections in the mirror.

"I'm the same girl you've always known." Fear raced through me. I didn't recognize the elegant woman standing beside Everly: the graceful sweep of her chignon, the diamonds draped around her neck, or the tightness about her eyes. Where had I gone? Each passing day swept me further and further from the girl I'd been and closer to someone new, a stranger in an upside-down world.

"No. You're not. You're so much more." Sadness tugged her lips downward. "Things are changing for both of us, Rourke."

"Why can't we stay the way we are?" I took the paper

towel from her and dabbed at the corners of my eyes. "I don't belong anywhere. I don't belong *here*."

"That's baloney. You belong here as much or more than anyone else." She leaned back to gain perspective on my appearance. With an affectionate touch, she smoothed a loose strand of hair back from my face. The warmth in her touch restored my faith in our relationship. "Much better."

"I can't go back out there." Butterflies fluttered in my stomach at the thought of facing Roman again. Before Everly had interrupted us, I'd been two seconds from dragging him onto the elevator and up to his room for a sex fest. And where would that leave us?

"Nonsense. You can be my date." She smiled and reapplied gloss to her pink mouth.

"Where's Nicky?" As soon as the words left my mouth, I bit my lower lip. Everly's expression chilled.

"He had to leave—a business engagement." When I swallowed and opened my mouth, she lifted a warning finger. "Don't you dare say it."

"You really believe him?"

Her lips pressed together in a stubborn line. "I choose to give him the benefit of the doubt. People can change, Rourke, whether you want to believe it or not."

"A leopard doesn't change his spots. If I were you, I wouldn't trust Nicky out of my sight." My anger with Roman bubbled up and spilled out, venting on Everly.

"Oh, great. Here we go again. You're the pot calling the kettle black. At least Nicky doesn't finance international warfare." Her verbal blow caught me squarely in the gut. I winced. She lifted her chin and backed away. "I can't deal with your judgmental bullshit tonight. I've got five hundred guests to think of."

"Don't worry. I'm leaving." Through a blur of tears, I rustled in my clutch for my phone and texted Lance for the car. "Just don't come crying to me when he fucks you over. Oh, wait. He's already fucking you over, and you don't even realize it."

Inside the limo, I fought back tears of anger and frustration. I'd lost control of my relationships, career and future. If something didn't change, I was going to lose my mind too.

CHAPTER 5
ROURKE

An hour later, I climbed into my giant bed—alone. My anger had burned down to ash, leaving me cold and ashamed. With a shiver, I tugged the blankets up to my chin. My iPhone rested on the nightstand beside me. I stared at it, willing Roman to call or text, but it remained conspicuously silent. What a fine mess. My husband was sleeping in a strange bed. My best friend hated me. Come to think of it, I kind of hated myself, too.

I picked up the phone and typed out a quick text to Everly: *I'm sorry.* She didn't reply, and I didn't blame her. Before I could message Roman, I dropped the phone in the drawer and closed it. My lips burned from his kiss. The space between my legs throbbed and pulsed with need. Maybe I should have gone back to his room with him. Sex had never been one of our problems and wouldn't solve our relationship issues, but it might have taken the edge off the constant ache of desire. Instead, I'd been too stubborn to concede. At this rate, we'd never come to any kind of truce. My pride wouldn't let me back down. He was in the wrong, not me. He should be the one to apologize.

When the sun came up, I dressed and went downstairs for breakfast. The chef, startled by my early appearance, hastily prepared a light breakfast of eggs and toast. If Ivan had been here, he would have known what to do, but he was gone—murdered by an assassin's bullet meant for my husband. Worry tied the muscles of my neck and shoulders into knots. Roman had seemed unraveled last night, and I needed to make sure he was safe.

Mother Nature, however, had other plans. Halfway through breakfast, I bolted to the bathroom and heaved up the contents of my stomach.

I stared at my pale reflection in the mirror. I was naturally fair, but my skin was deathly white. My stomach bucked as a second wave of nausea rolled through me. When the threat of more upheaval passed, I brushed my teeth, rinsed my mouth, and found the calendar app on my phone. My last period had been six weeks ago. I counted the days again. Until our separation, Roman and I had been fucking like love-starved maniacs. Although I'd never missed a birth control pill, they weren't 100% effective. It *was* possible.

After the shock died down, I swore one of the staff members to secrecy and sent her out for a pregnancy test. To pass the time while waiting for her return, I showered and dressed. When she knocked on the bedroom door and handed the drugstore bag to me, I ran to the bathroom, peed on the stick, and stared at the tiny display window. Two minutes later, the timer on my phone buzzed. A blue plus sign faded into view. She'd purchased two; I took the second test. Definitely a plus sign. Definitely pregnant.

I pressed a hand to my somewhat-flat belly, closed the lid on the toilet, and sat down to assess my feelings. Pictures of Roman holding a little boy with his dark, wavy hair or a little girl with long blond curls flashed through my head. The scene flooded me with warmth. He was a wonderful father to Milada, even though she wasn't his biological child. The warmth gave way to cold panic. His words from our first meeting at the Masquerade de Marquis fought their way through my memories. *"My friends say I'm the devil."* He'd tried to warn me off that night, but I'd been swept away by his mystique and the glint of desire in his eyes. Look where it had landed me—squarely in hell.

When I was able to collect my composure, I called Everly. Even though she hadn't replied to my text, she was my only family. Times like these called for girl power. I needed her level-headed sensibility to reel me back from the brink of panic.

She answered on the last ring before the call went to voice mail. "I can't talk to you right now," she said, in a thick, nasally voice.

"What's wrong?" Alarm bells rang in my head. I clutched the phone tighter, fearing the worst. "Are you okay?"

"No." She hiccupped.

"Are you sick? Want me to call the doctor?"

"No. I just—" Her words ended in a choked sob.

"I'm coming over, and I won't take no for an answer. Hold tight, sweetie." I dropped my phone into my purse and dashed downstairs to find Lance. The sight of his calm, unsmiling face soothed my nerves. "Can you get the car? I need to go to Ms. McElroy's apartment. It's urgent."

"Certainly." He swept an arm toward the elevator. On the way, he texted my driver. Once the elevator doors had closed and the car began its descent, he studied me. His eyes filled with compassion. "Is everything okay, ma'am?"

"No." Tears burned the backs of my eyelids. I blinked them away and straightened my shoulders. A breakdown was a luxury I couldn't afford.

The elevator doors opened. We rode down to the ground floor in silence. Through the tall glass windows of the building entrance, the rising sun glistened on the chrome trim of my car as it pulled to the curb. Quiet enveloped the inside of the Maybach. I ran a hand over the luxurious fawn-colored leather. Fancy cars had never been my thing, but Roman had insisted on the gift. When I'd protested, he'd waved a hand through the air. "I replace all my cars every year, Rourke. It's procedure. Not everything is about you." The twinkle in his eye had suggested otherwise.

I wrapped my arms around my waist. Even when I was furious with him, I yearned for his embrace, to smell his spicy cologne, and to hear his deep voice.

Fifteen minutes later, I arrived at Everly's apartment. She opened the door, gaze downcast. Right away, I noticed her puffy eyes. Lance waited in the hallway while I went inside. She'd only lived there a few weeks, but the place already bore the marks of her good taste. White walls, comfortable, over-stuffed furniture, and pale-blue accents provided a calming effect. I pulled her into a tight hug. My drama with Roman would have to wait. "Talk to me."

She sniffed, hiding behind her tissue. "It's so stupid. I didn't want to say anything, because you told me so."

"Nicky?" Her head bobbed up and down. My heart squeezed for her. "What did he do? I swear I'm going to kill him." Fierce feelings of protectiveness welled inside me. She was my tribe. No one had the right to hurt her, especially a bastard like Nicky.

"He—he—he said he had last-minute business. And then I saw this." After swiping away the moisture on her cheeks, she flashed her phone screen in front of me. Photos of Nicky at the opening of a new Soho nightclub with a young, glamorous starlet, time stamped for last night. "I thought maybe it was a mix-up or a publicity stunt, but one of my friends said she saw them there. They were definitely a couple." Her shoulders sagged. "I'm such an idiot."

"No, you're not. You're kind and beautiful and smart and way too good for him." I swept her hair away from her face. "Any man who doesn't recognize how fabulous you are doesn't deserve you."

"I'm sorry I yelled at you last night." Her hand found mine and squeezed. "I realized this morning I'm *that* girl—the kind I used to complain about—the one who always picks the wrong guy then cries about it."

"Have you asked him to explain?" Although my head insisted the photograph reflected the truth, my heart wanted to believe otherwise, for Everly's sake.

She nodded. "I went to his apartment this morning, and she was there. He didn't try to deny it or anything. He just shrugged, like he didn't care. I was so humiliated." I drew her into another hug, fighting back the sting of empathetic tears. "You know what burns my ass the most? The whole time he was with her last night, he was texting me, pretending like I'm special when I'm really not."

"Oh, Everly. I'm so, so sorry." I stroked her hair, wishing I could absorb the pain for her. "At least you're not pregnant by a Russian warlord."

The morning sunlight reflected in her tears as her eyes went wide. "Are you joking?"

"No. I'm serious. I've got a bun in the oven."

"Did you pee on a stick?"

"Twice." Tears welled in her eyes again, and we both began to cry. No wonder I'd been so emotional lately. My hormones were all over the place.

"Oh, sweetie, that's wonderful. And I'm a little bit jelly, because that big, hot man stud of yours knocked you up. It *is*

Roman's, isn't it?" She held me at arm's length and cocked an eyebrow.

I shoved her shoulder playfully. "Of course."

"Just asking. I know how you like to get freaky at the club." Her lips smiled, but her eyes remained glassy. She sniffed and dabbed at her nose with a tissue.

"Stop. You know it's his." We laughed; something I hadn't done in weeks.

"I'm going to be crazy Auntie Everly. I'll teach her or him how to curse and spit and smoke cigarettes—"

"You don't smoke or spit." I rolled my eyes at her but smiled. She personified the epitome of etiquette and good taste.

"Kidding. I swear." She lifted two fingers in an approximation of a scout pledge and placed her other hand over her heart. "Seriously, you're going to be a fantastic mom."

Mom. I was pregnant with Roman Menshikov's baby. A slow, secretive smile stretched my mouth, followed by the warmth of pride. If only my mother, who'd believed in fairytales, could see her daughter now. The excitement faded as reality returned. I sank down on the couch, overcome by the exhaustion of the past month, and shook my head. "This couldn't have happened at a worse time."

"It seems like the perfect time to me." Worry drew her eyebrows together. "You're—you're going to have it, right?"

The option to terminate the pregnancy had never occurred to me. I placed a defensive hand on my stomach. Fierce feelings of loyalty and protection burned in my veins. "Absolutely. This baby means the world to me."

"It's clearly a sign from God that you need to get your ass over to your man and make up."

"It's not that simple."

Taking my arm, she drew me to the sofa and onto the plush cushions. "It's only as complicated as you make it. If you want to be with him, make it happen. Have you thought about seeing a counselor?"

I rolled my eyes. "Right. Can you imagine? 'My husband and I are having difficulty adjusting to our new life as a married couple. And, did I mention that he's a war lord?'"

"Okay. Maybe not."

"He's in some kind of trouble." I spoke slowly, choosing my words with care. Divulging unnecessary details might put her in harm's way, something I couldn't risk. Until I knew more about Roman's situation, caution was imperative. Instead, I gave her the broad points of the story. "Someone is threatening him, I think." Speaking the words aloud gave our predicament gravity. "I'm scared, Everly."

We stared at each other. Her clear-blue eyes sharpened. "Roman's a smart man. I'm sure he has everything under control." She patted my hand. "Mom said you're coming to dinner tonight. You can ask Daddy. He knows everyone's secrets." Her eyes narrowed. "What about you? You seem to have plenty of secrets yourself."

"No—well, maybe. You remember the time I called off work when we were in Paris a few years ago? I wasn't sick. I went to the hotel bar the night before, hooked up with a guy, and had a horrible hangover the next morning." I grinned, trying to lighten the mood.

"You told me you had food poisoning. I'm impressed." Her smile brightened. "As long as we're confessing, I might have borrowed your favorite blue sweater in high school and never returned it."

"Are you kidding me? You know how hard I hunted for it, and you never said a word." The humor of the moment faded. I sobered and the smile fell from my lips. "No more secrets. You're the only person I've got, Everly. I need you."

"Absolutely." She extended her little finger, the same way she had when we were seven years old. "Pinky swear."

Memories of hopscotch, dollhouses, and Malibu Barbie burned in my heart at the gesture. I curled my finger around hers. "You're the best." Through the deaths of my parents and her divorce, we'd managed to remain close. I wouldn't let Nicky Tarnovsky come between us. She was my best friend, and I'd protect her to my dying breath.

CHAPTER 6
ROURKE

With Lance at my side, I left Everly's building and headed toward the car. During my visit, heavy clouds had moved across the city, obscuring the sun and casting the tall buildings into shadow. Numbness descended over my emotions while my mind raced with endless questions about Roman, his secret life, and our impending parenthood. Having a child bound us together for eternity. There was no escaping him now—*if* I wanted to escape.

Two paces from the car, Lance stepped in front of me, shielding my body with his. Startled out of my reverie, I glanced up. A middle-aged, balding man in a tan suit approached with rapid footsteps. As he walked toward me, his right hand disappeared inside his jacket. Lance shoved me into the open car, slamming the door behind me.

I toppled onto the cool leather seat and let out a startled, "Oof!"

The man withdrew a badge and ID from his inside suit pocket and held it up to the car window, his voice muffled through the glass. "Mrs. Menshikov, I'm Federal Agent

Timothy Frankel. I need to speak with you about your husband."

Lance placed a hand on the man's chest and shoved him back a pace. "Go, go," Lance urged the driver.

"No. Wait." I held up a hand and weighed the merits of speaking to him. Although I didn't want to incriminate Roman, this man might provide important clues to my husband's secrets. I rolled down the window. "It's okay, Lance."

"Can we go somewhere and talk—alone?" Frankel returned his ID to his pocket but not before throwing an irritated glare in Lance's direction. "How about your place?"

"No," Lance said, his brow furrowing. "Absolutely not."

I pushed the car door open. "If you want to speak with me, get in. Lance, you sit back here with us."

"Alright." Frankel slid into the vacant seat across from me.

Lance followed him into the car. "For the record, Mrs. Menshikov, I don't like this."

"It's okay, Lance," I said.

"Give me your gun." He extended a hand toward the agent. After a moment's hesitation, the man removed his pistol from the holster inside his suit coat and handed it, butt first, to Lance. He placed the weapon on the seat beside him and turned to the driver. "Take us around the park. Make sure we aren't followed. If this guy does anything out of line, you know what to do."

The ominous note of warning in his command made my hands tremble. I clasped them together, not wanting the agent to see my fear.

The driver nodded, lifted the partition, and merged into traffic.

"What can I do for you?" I forced my features into a neutral expression. Panic sharpened my senses. The details of his appearance washed over me. A tiny scar on his forehead.

Pock marks on his cheeks. Bushy, dark eyebrows. He smelled of cheap cologne, but the lines of his expensive suit had been tailored to fit his trim build, suggesting a taste for the finer things in life. The thin sole of his left shoe showed when he rested an ankle on his knee. Maybe his lifestyle outpaced his bank account.

"I'm investigating the death of Lavender Cunningham," he said, leveling his flat gaze on mine. "Can you tell me about the last time you saw her?"

"We had a meeting to discuss arrangements for one of Roman's social events." Had it really only been a month? It seemed like a lifetime ago. In the blur of recent events, I'd completely forgotten about Lavender and the Masquerade de Marquis. "That was the only time we'd ever met in person."

"Were you aware she'd had a longstanding relationship with your husband?"

"Yes." With forcible effort, I unclenched my fingers and drew in a breath, getting a mouthful of Aqua Velva. I exhaled through my nose, fighting back a rising tide of nausea. "They have a business affiliation."

"Really? Is that what they're calling it these days?" Sarcasm dripped from his voice. "Did he also tell you about his monthly deposits into her checking account, the Upper East Side apartment he had purchased for her, the cars, the vacations? I can go on, if you'd like. There's a lot more."

The scent of his cologne intensified and stirred the contents of my stomach. *I will not throw up. I will not throw up.* I mentally repeated the words and tried to breathe through my mouth. Roman had told me about a past dalliance with Lavender, but vacations and cars suggested something much deeper than a fling. I resisted the claw squeezing my heart and lifted my chin. How should I answer his question? If I said no, I'd look like a fool. If I acknowledged the affair, then I might be implicating myself. A scorned wife had plenty of reasons to cause harm toward her husband's mistress. I decided to hedge my bets and stick to short answers. "I trust him."

He shook his head, pityingly. "You don't seem stupid, but I can't understand why you'd let him support a mistress right beneath your nose." His gaze narrowed. "Unless you married him for his money and were relieved to get him off your back?"

My temper itched beneath my skin, begging to be unleashed on this douchebag. Instead, I pressed the button to crack the car window and took a gulp of city air. "Is this why you wanted to talk? So you could question my motives for marrying Roman? If it is, then you're wasting my time and yours."

"I'm trying to figure out who might have killed Ms. Cunningham. Was it the eccentric billionaire wanting to get rid of a pain-in-the-ass mistress? Or his jealous wife?"

"I thought it was a suicide," I said, relaxing as the nausea subsided and my head cleared.

"So did local law enforcement until her ties with the Russian mafia were unearthed. That's where I come in. You see, Ms. Cunningham's real name was Olga Walenska. She and your husband go way, *way* back. Back to his childhood."

Betrayal knifed my chest. I covered my surprise with a pleasant smile. Roman had never mentioned his connection to her beyond their working relationship. Why hadn't he told me? "I'm afraid I don't have the answers you're looking for." All the while, my blood simmered with the urge to punch him for giving me another reason to question my marriage. "Why don't you ask my husband?"

"I'd love to, but he seems to have left the Four Seasons. Do you know where I can find him?"

"If you can't find him, then you must not be very good at your job." My breakfast churned in my stomach. A strong sense of fight-or-flight lifted the hairs on the back of my neck. I swallowed hard. Perhaps I'd underestimated Agent Frankel's abilities to get beneath my skin.

He studied my face. "You're white as a sheet. Are you feeling well?"

"I'm fine." Nothing could have been farther from the truth. I bit the inside of my cheek to keep from defending Roman and myself. Frankel was trying to bait me, and I wouldn't give in to his bullying.

Taking my silence as agreement, he continued, his words gathering speed and volume. "I know you're living separately. Are you having problems? Did he tell you about Lavender? Is that why you split up? Everyone will understand if you're angry with him—or with Lavender. Did you argue? Talk to me, Mrs. Menshikov. Maybe I can help. Tell us what you know, and I can offer you immunity."

"From what?" My panic escalated.

Frankel said nothing, his stare burning through me. Lance glanced between us.

I lowered the driver partition. "Stop the car, please. Agent Frankel is getting out." And then I vomited on his shoes.

☙❧

WE LEFT AGENT FRANKEL STANDING ON THE CURB AT Central Park West and Eighty-First Street. Through my misery, I caught a glance at his opened mouth and lowered brows as the car resumed traveling. If I hadn't been completely miserable, I would've laughed.

"Are you okay?" Lance withdrew a packet of disposable wipes from the console and handed them to me. "Do you need a doctor?"

"No." I wiped my hands and mouth. "I mean, yes, I'm fine. I should have something to eat. I'll be better in a minute." In fact, the tide of nausea ebbed with each passing second.

He chuckled. "I'd pay good money to see you puke on that guy again."

"Well, if I don't get some food in my stomach, your shoes might be next." While he disposed of the mess on the floor, I dug through the small cabinet next to the mini-fridge for crackers. I nibbled around the edges, gingerly, waiting for any signs of gastric rebellion. "Thank you."

"You handled him well." Lance handed me a bottle of water and settled back into his seat. "I'm impressed."

"Really?"

"Yeah. He's just trying to goad you into giving up information. If they had any evidence at all, they would've hauled both of you in already."

"True." I rested my forehead against the cool window. Had Roman's problems been a result of Lavender's murder? Was he somehow mixed up with the Russian mafia? A new, more horrifying thought took shape. What if *he* was the Russian mafia?

"Forgive me for overstepping, but if you know anything about Mr. Menshikov, you might want to consider Frankel's offer."

"Yes, I do mind." The option of betraying Roman had never occurred to me. Even if I knew his secrets, I'd never divulge them. "If I want your opinions, I'll ask for them." I'd never spoken harshly to an employee, but I refused to feel guilty. Like it or not, I was married to Roman. He deserved my loyalty for the sake of our wedding vows and our unborn child. "I don't mean to be rude, but you can't say things like that."

"Of course. I apologize." He leaned back in the seat, his gaze assessing.

After a swallow of water, I dug in my purse for my phone.

It wasn't there. I mentally scrolled back through the morning, trying to think of the last time I'd had it.

"Is something wrong?" Lance's brow furrowed.

"My phone. I could have sworn it was in my purse." I squirmed on the seat, trying to see if it had fallen into one of the cracks.

"Here it is. You must have dropped it when you got in the car." He slipped a hand between the door and the seat, withdrew my phone, and handed it to me.

When we returned to the penthouse, I went straight upstairs and took a long, soothing bath. The water eased away the tension in my muscles. Nothing, however, could take away the anxiety in my heart.

CHAPTER 7
ROMAN

TWENTY YEARS EARLIER...

"Roman, come." From the front steps of our house, my father called to me.

I tossed the football back to Nicky then wiped my palms on the thighs of my jeans. Bright sunlight impeded my view. I lifted a forearm to shield my eyes. While I'd been absorbed in a game of pass with my younger brother, a black sedan had parked in the driveway. The driver exited the car and joined my father.

"Do you remember me, Roman?" A Russian accent gave his words sinister intent.

"Yes. You're Ivan." This man had hovered on the periphery of the major events in my life: family reunions, school functions, and birthdays. I'd never questioned his appearance, because he'd always been there.

"Good." Ivan nodded. His black suit and slicked-back hair seemed more fitting for an undertaker than a family friend.

I glanced over at my father, uncertain.

"Is okay," he said in his broken English. "You speak with him."

Most of my father's acquaintances visited under cover of darkness, speaking Russian in hushed tones and drinking vodka by the gallon. This man seemed more refined, a curious mixture of elegance and brutality in his sharp features.

"You've grown since the last time I saw you," he said. We shook hands. I squared my shoulders, almost able to look him in the eyes. At fifteen, I was already six feet tall and building muscle. Something sparked in his gaze. "You look very much like your father."

"You must need glasses," I said, making him snort. My father's sandy-brown hair and gray eyes contrasted sharply with my black hair and blue eyes. Before now, I'd never questioned our physical differences. My gaze fell on Nicky, who shared our father's features and coloring, standing in the middle of the yard, football clutched beneath his arm. "I take after my mother."

"Come inside, Roman," my father said. "We must talk. Nicky, you also."

The four of us gathered around the kitchen table. Marie, our housekeeper, poured coffee for the men. She smiled at me, patted my shoulder, and placed a bottle of Coke on the table. The hairs on the back of my neck lifted in premonition. Soft drinks were reserved for weddings, funerals...and bad news.

"Can I have a Coke too?" Nicky asked, rocking back on the heels of his chair beside me.

"No. Will rot your teeth." Father gave him a pointed glance of reproach. "Stop rocking chair."

Nicky frowned and lowered the chair to the floor.

"It's time, Roman," Ivan said. "Time for you to know the truth about who you are and our plans for you."

I wasn't sure where he was going with this line of conver-

CHAPTER 8
ROURKE

PRESENT DAY...

Later that evening, I joined Everly and her parents at their Fifth Avenue townhouse for dinner. The McElroys greeted me with warm hugs and smiles, in the foyer beneath the coffered ceilings and enormous chandeliers. Their stately mansion, with its dark wood paneling and classic furnishings, felt like home. Mrs. McElroy looped an arm through mine, leading me toward the dining room. The heavy diamond bracelet on her wrist rubbed against my bare forearm. The barest hint of perfume hovered around her. I swallowed down a nostalgic lump in my throat. Being here reminded me of all their many kindnesses throughout my life.

Mr. McElroy pulled out a chair for me in the dining room. "It's wonderful to see you again, Rourke."

"You mustn't be a stranger," Mrs. McElroy interjected. "We've missed you." She nodded to the waitstaff for the meal to begin. Someday, when I was less preoccupied with my crazy life, I planned to ask her for tips on the seamless way she ran her household. Her hand found mine across the table. "I was so sorry we couldn't make it to your Aunt May's funeral. She was a wonderful woman, and your mother loved her so much. I want you to know you're always welcome here. You're like family to us."

I smiled, grateful for her generosity. "I feel the same way."

"I think a toast is in order. It's been too long since we've had you at our table." Mr. McElroy's blue gaze homed in on my face, causing me to flush with warmth. He lifted his wine glass. "To Rourke."

"Thank you." I lifted the wine glass to my lips, took a sip, then remembered my newfound motherhood. Surreptitiously, I pretended to take a longer drink and let the wine trickle back into the glass. Goodness, what was wrong with me? Only one day into my pregnancy, and I was already slipping up. Everly's eyebrows lifted, and she cleared her throat to hide a chuckle. I shrugged.

"We have so much to catch up on. I want to hear all about your wedding. How did you meet Roman Menshikov?" Mrs. McElroy's eyes lit up. In size and coloring, she resembled Everly. Her graying red hair had been swept into a low chignon, and the pale blue of her suit highlighted her eyes. "Such a handsome man and so mysterious. He's always been one of the largest contributors to my foundation for homeless children."

"Well..." Choosing my words carefully, I gave her a sanitized version of the truth but omitted any mention of the Masquerade de Marquis and the chain of Devil's Playground sex clubs. She and her husband listened, nodding occasionally. They'd always been attentive, and both had a way of making a person feel important. It was one of the reasons they'd come so far in the world of politics. Before Mr. McElroy became Vice President, Mrs. McElroy had been a state senator. They were a shining example of a good marriage between two powerful people. Maybe it was possible to create a similar relationship with Roman. *If* he ever got out of this mess he'd created.

Following the meal, we retired to one of the sitting rooms. On the way there, Mr. McElroy drew me into his study. My mouth went dry as he closed the door behind us. I chased back the fear and gave him a tremulous smile. The tiny lines around his eyes and mouth had deepened, and his thick hair had gone from salt-and-pepper to silver, but he looked like the same man I'd learned to love and respect as a kid. I was safe here.

"I won't mince words with you, Rourke. I wanted to speak with you last night but never had the chance to get you in private. I'm worried about you. Your husband's in deep shit." The ominous tone of his words made my mouth grow dry. He withdrew a cigar from an elaborate antique humidor. The room filled with the scent of tobacco. "Do you mind? I know I should quit, but Judy has pretty much put a stop to all my bad habits, and a man needs some kind of vice."

"No, it's fine." I drew in a tentative breath, hoping the smell didn't resurrect my morning sickness, but the aroma reminded me of when my father used to sit around the fireplace with Mr. McElroy and swap stories about their college days.

"Anyway—" He paused long enough to clip the end of the cigar and lit it. "Roman backed out on a business deal with some of my associates. They're very displeased."

"He doesn't discuss the particulars of his business with me." My gut warned me to play innocent, while my head wanted to defend my husband. I shifted uncomfortably, unnerved by the undercurrent of tension in the room. For some reason, I felt like a juvenile delinquent in the principal's office. My palms began to sweat.

"I've got to tell you, Rourke. I'm afraid for your safety."

He gave my shoulder a fatherly pat. I flinched at his touch. "I really think you need to consider annulment or divorce. There's no shame in putting an end to an unsavory situation. You just got in over your head with this man. Hell, we all make mistakes. Look at Everly. She married that Australian chap and went through hell because of it. Lucky for you, I can help you get out of this mess." He moved to the liquor cabinet and poured bourbon into a short glass. "Would you like some?"

"None for me, thanks." I shook my head, fighting off panic. If I wanted out of my marriage, here was my opportunity. The thought made my insides quake. I placed a hand on my belly, remembering the tiny life growing there—the one Roman and I had created. Our child deserved a chance at two loving parents.

"Do you have a prenup?" Mr. McElroy's shrewd gaze caught mine, gleaming with interest.

"Um, we have provisions in place." An hour ago, I'd have confided the details of our financial agreement to Mr. McElroy, but he was too intent on my expression. Maybe I was being paranoid. He was America's hero, after all. I tried to relax. The events of the past month had made me suspicious of everyone.

"Good. Smart girl. No matter what happens, you'll be financially set. My lawyers can handle all the details. Should I set something up?" Wisps of smoke curled around his head while he waited for my answer.

I gave him a tight smile and stood. "Oh, my goodness. I had no idea it was so late. Can we continue this conversation another time? I've got to get back home." Mustering a serene smile, I patted his arm. "Thank you so much for your hospitality. Will you excuse me? I'd better say goodbye to Everly and your wife before I go."

I fled before he could ask more questions. Everly gave me

a sympathetic smile as she walked me to the door. I longed to confide in her, but the words lodged in my throat. Until I knew more about Roman's situation, I had to keep my mouth shut. I wouldn't be manipulated into betraying my husband by Mr. McElroy or anyone else.

CHAPTER 9
ROURKE

The next day, unable to face the emptiness of the penthouse, I went to the office for distraction. Mr. McElroy's unexpected offer refused to stop rattling through my head. He'd given me the perfect escape to the mess I'd found myself in, and yet, I'd been unable to take it. The reason stared me in the face. I'd loved Roman from the night we'd met at the Masquerade de Marquis. No other man would ever be able to satisfy me. He was my one and only, and I'd never, ever end our marriage.

The sight of his empty desk made my fragile stomach quiver. I ignored the curious gazes of the employees and took a seat in his chair. The cool leather sent a chill up my back. Even in absentia, his presence dominated the room. His coffee cup sat on the corner of his desk, empty and forlorn. Traces of his cologne drifted from the sweater draped over the back of his chair. He was everywhere, all the time, but mostly, he was in my head and heart. I picked up the gold-framed portrait on the corner of the desk. Roman's arm wrapped around Milada's shoulders. She smiled up at him adoringly. Sitting here in his chair, behind his oversized desk, made me feel closer to him.

What was I going to do? Options collided and tumbled over each other, none of them gaining a foothold. We could live separately, a choice Roman would never accept. Could I concede to his dangerous lifestyle in order to save our marriage? With a heavy sigh, I powered up my laptop and began mindlessly sorting through my emails. Three of them came from Lavender Cunningham's replacement. I tagged them for later, unable to face the details of the Masquerade de Marquis now.

"Mrs. Menshikov?" One of Roman's executive assistants popped her head through the open door. "May I speak with you for a moment?"

"Um, sure." I closed the email screen and swiveled the chair to face her. Although my emails weren't particularly sensitive in nature, I wasn't sure who I could trust anymore. "What can I do for you?"

After a hasty glance down the hallway, she stepped into the office and closed the door behind her. Threads of premature gray glistened in her dark-brown hair. Fine lines around her eyes suggested she was in her early forties. She didn't return my tentative smile. "There are rumors going around the office, and I thought maybe I should confront you directly instead of listening to speculation."

"Oh?" Of course, people had questions. I'd been around the corporate environment long enough to understand the way gossip ignited and swept through a building like wildfire.

"Yes." She wrung her hands in front of her, a slight blush coloring her freckled skin. "You know how facts get exaggerated."

"I'm glad you came to me first, Lorissa," I said. "Please, have a seat." Meanwhile, beneath my calm exterior, my heart thudded against my chest. Had she heard about Roman's detainment? His PR staff had been working overtime to squelch the damage done by Ivan's assassination. I made a mental note to check in with them before I left.

"Is everything okay with Mr. Menshikov?" Her blush deepened, extending to the tips of her ears. My jaw dropped. She raised a palm toward me. "It's really no one's business but your own, and I—"

"Yes, you're right," I replied, cutting her off mid-sentence. Inside, I breathed a sigh of relief. I could handle these kinds of rumors. "What, specifically, do you want to know?"

"I apologize again for overstepping, but you haven't been to work in weeks. And Mr. Menshikov has seemed so very... melancholy lately." When I didn't stop her, the words tumbled from her mouth. "Last week, I asked him to sign a couple of contracts, and he put his signature on the wrong line. *Twice.* I've worked with him for six years. Mr. Menshikov has never done that. *Never.*"

An unfamiliar twist tightened my chest. All this time, I'd been too caught up in my feelings to consider his. He'd been hurting just as much as me.

She lowered her voice. "And he hasn't yelled at me in days. Not once. I've been trying to get hold of him this morning, and he hasn't returned any of my texts or voicemails. Usually, he's calling and texting me twenty-four seven."

I tried not to laugh at her accurate depiction of his megalomaniac behavior. "You're worried about him." The tension eased from my muscles. Half the female staff had a crush on my husband, and who could blame them? He was exotic and mysterious and handsomer than any man had a right to be.

"Yes. I just—just wanted to make sure he was okay." Her gaze flitted from the floor to mine. "Is he?"

"He's fine," I said, shocked by how easily the lie slipped

from my tongue. "He's dealing with a sensitive business deal right now and has spotty cell service, but I'm sure he'll get back to you as soon as he can."

"That's good to know." Her shoulders dipped, and her smile returned.

"As for my absence, I'm no longer Mr. Menshikov's assistant. My replacement is learning the ropes at our home. He should be into the office within the next week. Is there anything I can help you with until then?" I clasped my hands on the desk in front of me and gave her a serene smile.

"Um, well, maybe." The arches of her neatly groomed eyebrows shot toward her hairline. I'd never interfered in Roman's business dealings, aside from my assistant duties. "A man has been calling here. He's left a dozen messages since yesterday. He said it's imperative he speaks with Mr. Menshikov right away."

"Get me his name and number, and I'll take care of it." Thinking we were done, I took a sip of coffee.

"I remember his name. Henry Von Stratton—you know, like the Prince of Androvia? It's kind of hard to forget."

I sputtered, splashing coffee down the front of my dress. She grabbed a handful of tissues from the corner of the desk for me and watched as I dabbed at the stains. I cleared my throat and scrambled to regain my composure. "Great. If you'll give me his number, I'll make sure Roman—Mr. Menshikov—gets it."

"Knock, knock." Nicky rapped on the door frame. "Can I come in?" His tall form filled the opening. The diamonds in his cufflinks sparkled in the overhead lights. Without waiting for an answer, he sauntered into the room. His gaze wandered the length of Lorissa's figure and warmed in appreciation. "Good afternoon, Lorissa. You're looking lovely today."

"Thank you, Mr. Tarnovsky." The corners of her lips twitched in a secretive grin.

My eyes bulged. The nature of their relationship couldn't have been more obvious. Inside, I fumed. Not only had he been screwing over my best friend, he'd been doing it with Roman's executive assistant and who knew how many other women.

"The pleasure is all mine. Believe me."

At his cocky smirk, my sanity snapped. "Are you kidding me?" I banged a hand on the desk. "Lorissa, out."

"Um, yes, ma'am." The door clicked softly behind her as she raced out of the room.

"Uh-oh." Nicky took a step in retreat, still smiling.

I rose to my feet, rounded the corner of Roman's desk, and grabbed the sleeve of his charcoal pin-striped jacket. "We need to talk."

"Why are you staring at me like that?" He eased his arm out of my grasp and straightened the lines of his suit.

"You know why."

"Not really." He smiled at his reflection in the window while adjusting the collar of his lavender shirt. In true Nicky fashion, he wore a purple tie and matching pocket square, somehow managing to make the combination chic and masculine.

"You're sleeping with Lorissa."

"So?" He preened, running a hand through his hair and smoothing the strays.

"Isn't she a little old for you?" Not that age mattered, but it was the principle.

"You wouldn't know it to look at her, but that woman is an animal in bed." His low whistle split the air. "She can go for days, and she does this thing with her—"

"Stop. I don't want to know." I held up a hand between us and squeezed my eyes shut, bracing for his next disgusting comment.

"You're acting more and more like your husband." The line of his lips curved downward.

"With you around, it's no wonder he's always in a bad mood. You're incorrigible, and not in a good way."

He chuckled. "So dramatic. If I didn't know better, I'd say you're jealous."

"You seriously don't get it?" I squeezed between him and the floor-to-ceiling glass, demanding his attention. He shook his head. The scent of whisky and sex hovered beneath his cologne. "What did I tell you about Everly?"

"That she's an excellent dancer and a natural redhead? Which is true, by the way." Less than six inches separated us. From his greater height, he smiled down at me, gray eyes dancing.

"Don't play stupid." I poked an index finger twice into his chest then a third time for good measure. He was hard and solid as an oak tree.

"Ouch." With lightning reflexes, he grabbed my finger before I could poke him a fourth time and held it tightly in his fist. "Careful, princess."

"I warned you to be nice to her. I told you not to break her heart."

"I *was* nice to her—very, very nice." He waggled his eyebrows. "In fact, I treated her better than any of the women in my life. Poor girl just needed a real man to show her a little kindness—and a good fucking. Sex can solve so many of life's problems."

"Don't talk about her like she's one of your party girls." My rage escalated a notch, something I hadn't deemed possible until that moment. The dam holding back my emotions crumbled and fell into a heap of rubble. Nicky still held my right index finger, but my left hand was free. I drew it back, intending to give him a good smack across the face on Everly's behalf, but he caught my wrist in midair. I grunted in frustration, needing to take my feelings out on someone. "That's not how a real man acts. You led her on, lied to her, then cheated on her."

"It's what I do, Rourke. Why are you even acting surprised?" We glared at each other. I lifted my chin higher. His hold relaxed. A troubled crease marred his forehead. He released me completely and took two paces backward. Fresh air filled the space between us.

I drew in a deep, cleansing breath. "You hurt her." Tears blurred the room as I thought of the pain on Everly's face. "She didn't deserve that."

"My God, you really are pissed, aren't you?" The smug playfulness slipped from his expression.

"She's devastated. You pretended to care about her when she was at her most vulnerable."

"I wasn't pretending." The broad line of his shoulders drooped. He rested a hip on the edge of Roman's desk, his gaze downcast. "I like her. Truly."

"So you stood her up then slept with someone else?" The contrite expression didn't fool me. No one manipulated emotions and expectations better than Nicky. "Newsflash— that's not acceptable behavior for a gentleman."

"I've never claimed to be a gentleman. She'll hate me for a while, and then she'll move on. This way, there's no going back for either of us." A flash of genuine sadness aged his face beyond his years. I almost felt sorry for him. Then I remembered his talent for manipulating my emotions and braced my shoulders.

"Your logic never fails to amaze me. You do the most outrageous, horrific things and somehow make them sound noble."

"You know I'm right. Suppose we started a legitimate relationship. Eventually, I'd fuck things up, and she'd really be hurt. It's better to give her a little pain today than devastate her years from now."

Although I didn't agree with his method of delivery, I had to admit—in his own screwed-up way—he'd done her a favor. Eventually, he'd destroy her. He didn't have the emotional toolkit to deal with genuine feelings and had dealt with the issue the only way he knew how. "There are better ways to break up with someone. Did you ever think about having a talk with her?"

"You must be mistaking me for someone else. I don't do feelings." Beneath the silkiness of his voice lurked a gossamer thread of pain. "It's so much easier to blow them off."

"That's bullshit, and you know it." The air thickened until I could barely breathed. "You need to make this right."

He threw his head back and stared at the ceiling, like he was beseeching God for patience. "Did you hear what I just said? No."

I groaned, my temper tested to the limit by his insolence. "Either you make it up to her, or I'll convince Roman to cut you out of his life."

His gray eyes flashed with a show of anger equal to my own. "Go ahead. I dare you." One corner of his mouth curled up. "He would never do that."

"Oh really? You don't think so?" I mimicked his smirk. "Try me."

An irritated growl rumbled from his throat. "Fuck." He punched at the air. "Fine. I'll apologize."

Although his surrender filled me with triumph, I knew he hand't learned his lesson. I shook my head. "Someday, you're going to have to admit that your actions hurt people, Nicky." My gaze flickered to the picture of Milada, his unclaimed, biological child. Nicky's focus followed mine. "Haven't you ever loved anyone besides yourself?"

His eyes narrowed. "Not everyone in the world is meant

for a happily-ever-after, Rourke. Of all people, you should recognize that."

The statement hit me in the gut with more force than a punch. "Don't turn this around on me. We're talking about you." I shoved aside the brutal honesty of his statement. "I'm really disappointed in you."

"Well, that makes two of us then." By the hardening of his jawline, I'd found a vulnerable spot in his ego. He twitched the knot of his tie, avoiding my gaze. "I came to see if you're doing okay with Roman being...occupied elsewhere...but obviously, that was a bad idea."

"Wait a minute." I closed my eyes. When I'd opened them, he'd moved to one of the leather club chairs. "You knew about Roman?"

Nicky shrugged and stared at the empty space between us. He picked up a small sculpture on the coffee table and traced the curves of the woman's breasts with an elegant fingertip. "I hear things from time to time."

"You knew? And you did nothing to help him?" The top of my head threatened to explode from the force of my anger. I paced the width of the office with long, forceful strides.

He shrugged again. "Sure."

"Why didn't you tell me?"

"It's not my place. You've told me to butt out of your relationship a dozen times. Roman's a big boy. He can take care of himself."

The callousness of his words broke down the last of my defenses. I slumped into the nearest chair and buried my head in my hands. The walls of my chest tightened. I struggled to breathe and fought the urge to throw something. How had I gotten to this place in my life? "This is un-freaking-believable."

"Why? It's all pretty routine from where I'm standing." He took a seat in the chair across from me and rested one nonchalant ankle on top of his knee. "The feds haul him in. They make threats. Then they let him go. It's what they do. The government might hate him, but they need him more. It'll all work out. You'll see."

"How do you know that?"

"Well, I don't know exactly, but I'm fairly confident. Say, forty-sixty."

"Those aren't good odds."

"And yet, you married him anyway." He pursed his lips, considering. "Your entire situation is tragic, in my opinion. You're the sweet, trusting angel, and he's Satan, ruling the world's underbelly from his Park Place stronghold. I tried to save you, but you wouldn't listen to me."

"You make it sound like you're the knight in shining armor when we both know it isn't true." He plucked imaginary lint from his pant leg. If my accusation offended him, he didn't show it. "Your motives are never altruistic."

"Now you really *do* sound like your husband." After an exasperated roll of his eyes, he shifted to stand. "I'm bored with this. Unless you want to talk about something fun, I'm out of here."

"No. Wait. Please. I need your help."

"Well..." The petulance slid from his expression, and he eased back into the couch, stretching an arm along the backrest, happy to regain the upper hand in our meeting. "I'm not sure what I can do, but I'll give it a go. And—you'll owe me a favor."

"Done." Although I hated the idea of being in debt to him, my desperation stole precedence. "Why is Roman in so much trouble?"

"Your dear husband has pissed off a lot of people in high places with his little coup in Kitzeh. He'll have to make nice with them before they let him off the hook."

"Why is Kitzeh such a big deal?" The population of the entire country could fit in Manhattan with room to spare.

"Kitzeh might be small, but it provides easy access between Russia and a handful of third-world countries." When I failed to make the connection, he tapped a hand on the armrest of his chair. "Also, there's Androvia. You've heard of Prince Heinrich, right?"

"The playboy prince?" Heat raced into my face at the memory of the masked, blond voyeur who'd watched me with Roman at the Devil's Playground NYC. I didn't know much about the prince beyond his tabloid love affairs and flourishing Instagram account. Now, I'd heard his name twice within the space of ten minutes.

"When Henry's father dies, and that looks to be soon, he'll become king. He's got a lot of radical ideas to modernize the country. He's worried about a takeover once he gains the throne, as well he should. He's been flirting with your husband, seeking his assistance. If Roman and Henry join forces, they can effectively staunch the flow of illegal arms to the Middle East. That gives Roman and Henry unlimited power. A lot of bad men are threatened over the idea. War is big money. But all this goes away if Roman is out of the picture. If I was you, princess, I'd be nervous." His prediction sent a cold shiver down my spine. Oblivious to my fear, he glanced at the gleaming platinum watch on his wrist and winced. "Geesh. Would you look at the time. I'm late for my Thursday threesome."

I groaned. "Can't you even pretend to care?"

"No. Not in my nature." He rose, unfolding his long limbs gracefully. I followed him to the door. "It's been delightful seeing you again, Mrs. Menshikov." With an exaggerated flourish, he took my hand in his and bowed to kiss my knuckles. I snatched my hand away. His laughter rang through the room and into the reception area. "Call me. We'll do dinner."

"When hell freezes over," I said a little too loudly, and flushed at the stares. Oh well, I'd embarrassed myself before, and this probably wasn't the last time either. I drew in a deep breath and turned to Lorissa. "Can you call the head of Roman's PR department and ask her to come to his office?"

"Yes. Right away." A scarlet flush climbed up her neck. She kept her focus glued to the computer screen. "Um, Mrs. Menshikov, am I in trouble?"

I shook my head. "You can relax. Who you date is your own business."

"Yes, ma'am." She swallowed visibly and lifted her gaze to meet mine. "I wouldn't want to jeopardize my job. Mr. Menshikov has been wonderful to me."

"Right."

"No, really." After a quick glance from side to side, she leaned forward and lowered her voice. "When I first came to work here, I'd just gone through a terrible divorce. My ex-husband was stalking me. I was terrified. He'd broken into our apartment twice and threatened to kill me if I didn't come back to him. No one would help me. The police did nothing. But Mr. Menshikov, he took care of it."

I rolled my lips together, trying to read between the lines. "You mean, he hired someone to protect you?"

"No, ma'am. I mean, *he took care of it.*" She glanced down at her hands. "No one has seen my ex-husband in a few years. He just vanished. Disappeared." She snapped her fingers, making me flinch.

"I see." My hands trembled at the implication. Had Roman done the same with Lavender? I didn't want to think about it, so I corralled my emotions and shoved them into the deepest recesses of my psyche. "Did you get Von Stratton's phone number?"

"Yes. I emailed it to you, and I jotted it down here." She handed the phone message to me.

"Do me a favor and delete anything you have with his name on it—emails or messages. Make sure you empty your trash folders, too. If he calls again, please give him my cell number. That's all. Thanks, Lorissa." As soon as the door closed behind her, I shoved the note into my pocket. Then, I deleted all traces of the correspondence. Knowing Roman, he had strong firewalls, but I didn't want to take any chances.

CHAPTER 10
ROURKE

I worked through the day, taking solace in the monotony of familiar tasks. The PR team assured me they had the media under control and were working overtime to counteract any negative publicity. When everyone had left, I gathered my purse and jacket and texted Lance to have the car brought around.

I slipped into the backseat of the limo, relieved to have made it through another day, then gave a startled gasp. Roman's dark, glittering blue eyes stared back at me from the depths of the quiet interior. His folded jacket and tie rested on the seat beside him. He'd unbuttoned the throat of his crisp, white shirt to reveal the notch of his collarbone, one of my favorite places on his body.

"Good evening." His deep voice rumbled through the quiet of the car. My heart leaped at the sound.

"You scared the crap out of me." I settled into the seat across from him and tried to hide the way my entire body trembled by feigning anger. "What are you doing here? Spying on me?"

"I'm tired of waiting, Rourke. We need to settle things."

I concentrated on arranging the folds of my dress around my knees. "The way I see it, you're not in the position to give orders."

His hand crept across the distance between us. He threaded his fingers through mine. The warmth in his grip, the tentative caress of his skin against mine, made me lose my train of thought. "Cocky. I like it."

"No more games."

"I understand." His voice held a somber note. He brushed the pad of his thumb over the back of my hand. The caress turned my blood to molten lava. "What are your demands, Mrs. Menshikov?"

"Mr. McElroy wants me to file for an annulment or a divorce." I swallowed and looked away. "He says I'm in way over my head and that I need to get out."

His fingers tightened around mine. "Is that what you want?" When I didn't answer, he gave a gentle tug, pulling me across the seat to his side of the vehicle.

"I want my husband back. I want to walk down the street without being followed. I want everything to go back to the way it was." I bit my lower lip to cut off the words, hating the way my voice quavered.

"That's never going to happen, Rourke. When you stepped into my world, you gave up all those things. The sooner you accept that, the better you'll be able to cope."

"Do you hear yourself?" I snorted and tried to pull away without success. "I feel like I've landed in the middle of a John Clancy novel."

"Come back to me, and I'll do everything in my power to make you happy. Name your price." His grip tightened on my hand. "Unless it's too late?"

I stared at him, considering his words. Seconds of silence ticked past. What if he refused my request? If he said no, could I live without him? For the sake of our unborn child, I had to try. I gathered my courage. "Give it up."

"What? The money? The houses? My businesses?"

"The guns. I want you to stop." His power and strength had drawn me to him from the start. Being his wife exceeded my wildest dreams. Was I wrong to ask him to give up the things that made him Roman Menshikov?

"You don't know what you're asking."

"I know exactly what I mean."

"I don't think you do." His eyes narrowed, sending a thrill down my spine. "You're asking for the impossible. It would be easier for me to purchase the moon."

I lifted my chin, unwilling to compromise.

He shook his head and leaned back on the seat, stirring the subtle scent of his cologne. "There are too many people involved—too many wheels in motion. It's not just about us. Thousands of lives are at stake." When I didn't reply, he growled in frustration. "Fuck. Why do you have to be so stubborn?" The flat of his palm scraped over the stubble of his burgeoning beard. "I've been working my whole life toward one goal, and you want me to throw it all away."

"You asked, and that's my answer."

For the first time, his gaze left me to stare out the window at the city. The car paused for a stoplight. He contemplated a couple holding hands on the sidewalk. Their small dog danced at the end of a leash, circling their feet. A pang of loss struck me in the chest. That would never be us.

"You're not playing fair, Rourke." One corner of his mouth lifted higher. "And you have no idea how much that turns me on. Do you have a counteroffer?" The darkness of his gaze caused a pulse of excitement between my legs.

"I might be in a better position to negotiate if I had more facts."

"Excellent. Continue." He twirled a finger in the air

between us, the way he often did during his business meetings when the pace slowed.

"Agent Frankel says you killed Lavender Cunningham, or that you had a hand in her death. Is it true?" I held my breath, dreading his answer. His next words could change the course of our lives forever.

Taking my chin between his thumb and forefinger, he tilted my face toward his. I reluctantly lifted my gaze. In the shadows, his blue irises seemed black. "I have no knowledge of Lavender's death."

Frankel's accusations prickled beneath my skin, but Roman's direct gaze brimmed with sincerity. "Did you buy her cars and vacations and an apartment?"

"I believe the question you're asking is have I been unfaithful to you. And the answer is no. Not once. And I never will. If you believe I'd cheat on you, then you don't know me at all." He lifted my hand to his lips and began to kiss the tip of each finger. Pops of desire sizzled beneath my skin. "I have many faults, Rourke, but above all else, I'm loyal. I pledged to be faithful to you, and I'll never, ever break that vow."

The truth in his words rang through me. Roman's deceptions had always been by omission. The shades of right and wrong began to blur together. I watched his full lips worship my fingers and felt my resolve dissipating. "I don't know who to believe anymore."

"Lavender went through a financial rough patch a few years ago and came to me for help. I loaned her money, assumed the mortgage on her apartment, and gave her one of my old vehicles. She's been repaying the debt in monthly installments, but no one mentioned that, did they? As for the vacations, occasionally I took her along on some of my business trips to coordinate my social events while I looked for another personal assistant. But that was long before you came along. As soon as I became serious about you, I told her those trips were off the table, and we'd need to find a new solution to her debt repayment."

I looked away, staring out the car window, weighing his answers against the bullshit I'd been told by Frankel, McElroy, and Nicky. "I want to believe you, but it's hard for me to trust you, given the situation you're in."

"You can verify everything I've said through our accountants. She signed a contract, and the payments have been documented." Despite the dimly lit interior, I saw the way he'd flinched at my accusations. I hated hurting him, and I hated myself more for questioning his integrity.

"And what about that night in your study? The night before she died. You were yelling at her on the phone. I saw her name on your caller ID."

"Were you spying on me, Rourke?" His smile grew wider. "I've seriously underestimated you."

I shrugged. "The only way I can find anything out is to snoop."

"Ivan to spoke with her about the breach of confidentiality the day before she died. She didn't like it. She called me, pissed off, and gave me an earful. That's all there is to it."

"Frankel said you had longstanding ties. He said her real name was Olga something-or-other."

"Walenska," he corrected. "Her father was secretary to my father and was killed trying to protect him. Our families have been intertwined for centuries. It's the reason I've always felt responsible for her welfare." Lines of worry deepened across his forehead. "She's just one of many."

"Why couldn't you tell me that?" During my sleepless nights, I'd failed to contemplate the enormity of his reach and how many people might be affected by his actions. I was beginning to understand.

"I don't want to worry you with unimportant details." The

simplicity of his answer added to my frustration. He lifted his eyebrows, goading me into rebuttal.

"When you hide things from me, it makes me nervous. I'm constantly wondering when the other shoe is going to drop."

"You're overthinking things." His gaze darkened and dropped to my mouth. My breath stuttered. He licked his lower lip, like he could taste me. "Everything is fine."

"Things are not fine." Past events had demonstrated the scope of Roman's power, but even billionaire warlords had their limitations. "Federal agents are following our every move. Ivan and Lavender are dead. One of us might be next. That's not the kind of life I want for—for us." I almost spilled the news of my pregnancy but held back at the last second. Before I told him about the baby, I needed reassurance of his good intentions.

"I've already lost one of the most important people in my life. I'm not going to lose you, too." Sadness underscored his words.

At the mention of Ivan, we fell silent for a moment. He continued to caress the backs of my fingers with the pad of his thumb, stroking up and down, his touch light and gentle. The strength of his gaze remained unwavering.

"I need guarantees." He didn't know it yet, but we had three lives to consider now instead of two.

"Spoken like a true businesswoman." His chuckle rumbled through my ears. I loved his voice with all its layers and textures. "You have to trust me, Rourke. I've been playing this game for a very long time." The weariness in his voice stirred my sympathies.

"You've been through this kind of situation before?" I covered his hand with mine, stilling his caresses. He'd been fighting an enormous battle alone.

"My entire life."

I closed the gap between us. The smooth fabric of his trousers grazed my bare leg, sending an electric thrill into my center. In that moment of honesty, I realized I'd never grow tired of him, or bored, or dissatisfied. We just needed to find a path wide enough to accommodate both of us. "You're not alone, Roman. You have me."

"Do I, Rourke?" he asked, and dropped his mouth to mine.

CHAPTER 11
ROMAN

Rourke's kiss gutted me. The velvet softness of her lips rekindled feelings of longing and desperation. She released my hand and leaned toward the opposite side of the car. I let her go, not because I wanted to, but because she seemed to need the separation. As the Maybach glided across Manhattan, I focused on the city. Once, I'd seen endless opportunities amid the concrete and steel, but tonight...tonight, I saw potential danger and the evidence of all my shortcomings. I kept fucking up at every turn. We didn't speak again until the car stopped in front of our building.

"Can I come upstairs?" The words stuck in my dry throat. The drive had passed by too quickly. I needed more time. I needed more *her.* "I'd like a hot shower and to grab a few things from my study before I go."

"Of course." She didn't look at me when she spoke. The loss of eye contact hurt more than the blade of a well-honed knife.

Jose opened the car door and extended a hand to help Rourke exit. The bright streetlights spilled over the sidewalk contrasting with the sobriety of the night. He nodded, his gaze meeting mine as I unfolded my body, noting the stiffness in my joints. "Welcome home, sir," he said.

"Thank you, Jose." I shook his hand, appreciating his loyalty. He'd been with me longer than any of my other employees. "How's your wife doing?"

Surprise flashed through his gaze at my question. Had I always been such an asshole? "Fine, thanks to you. The doctors think they got all of the tumor, and she's headed toward remission."

"No need to thank me." Calling in a team of specialists to treat her cancer had been as simple as a phone call for me, but it meant the world to him. If I hadn't used my resources to help him, I'd never have forgiven myself. "Give her my best, would you?"

Rourke paused at the revolving door and glanced over her shoulder. "Roman? Are you coming?"

I tried not to read anything into the straight line of her lips. I couldn't remember the last time I'd seen her smile. Had I done that to her? Robbed the joy from her life? In the grand scheme of things, I didn't give a damn what the world thought of me. Only her. I never wanted to disappoint her, and I'd done nothing but let her down since our marriage.

We passed the security desk, our heels tapping on the pristine marble tiles. Inside the elevator car, I slid my key into the card reader for the penthouse. She stared straight ahead, hands clasped in front of her, chin raised. As we began our ascent toward the penthouse, my misgivings grew with each passing floor. I'd closed enough deals in my life to know when I was losing the contract. This was my strength; I crushed it in the boardroom. If I didn't act quickly, she might slip through my fingers again.

I pressed the stop button. The car lurched to a halt.

"What's wrong?" Her eyes widened. "Roman?"

"Fuck it," I said. Unlocking the sliding door that housed an invisible key pad on the control panel, I typed in the sequence of numbers that would reveal all my secrets. The elevator reversed directions.

"Where are we going?"

"Down."

"You promised no more games. I'm tired." The weariness in her tone bolstered my decision. We'd been tiptoeing around each other for too long. She puffed out a heavy breath. "I need to rest."

"You want answers. I'm giving them to you. This is me laying all my cards on the table. Full disclosure. I only need a few minutes."

She raised her eyebrows. "Alright. The floor is yours, Mr. Menshikov."

What I was about to do breached every level of security in my business, but it had to be done. If I was going to trust her—if she was going to make the transition from bystander to partner—she needed to know the stakes. I'd always been a gambler, and I was willing to place all my chips on her.

I inhaled and prepared to speak the words I'd never spoken to anyone. "When I was seventeen, Ivan took me to Kitzeh." I lifted a hand at her scowl. "I know I told you I'd never been there, but it wasn't a complete lie. Roman Menshikov has never been there. We toured the countryside under false names. I met the people of my country. They still spoke of my parents and what their legacy had meant to them." The memories of their rundown homes, their starving faces, and their hopelessness haunted my nightmares. "The new government promised them prosperity and peace but delivered poverty and terror."

"It must have been traumatic." Her hand touched mine. I was getting through to her. It became more important than ever to make her understand why Kitzeh meant so much to me.

"Everyone with the Menshikov name had been executed, but a few of my relatives hid, changed their identities, and continued to talk about reclaiming control of the country. I left with a new understanding of who I was and the gravity of my responsibilities." The pain of those days brought a lump to my throat. It felt good to share my history with her.

"I don't know what to say." Her fingers threaded through mine. I yearned to pull her close but hesitated, not wanting to lose the ground I'd gained.

"You don't need to say anything. I just wanted you to know." The elevator passed the ground floor and continued its descent, taking us into the heart of my hidden world. When the doors opened, there would be no turning back for either of us.

CHAPTER 12
ROURKE

The elevator doors opened into a vault-like room. Roman strode to the sliding metal doors on the far wall and gazed into a retina scanner on the wall. A green light flashed. Metal locks clicked. Sliding doors parted, revealing an observation deck.

"Come in." He beckoned me with a twitch of his fingers.

"Fuck me," I whispered. We stood in front of a glass wall overlooking a state-of-the-art command center. Below us, people milled between rows of computer monitors. Large flat-screen TVs covered the farthest wall, displaying satellite images. My heart began to clang against my ribs. "What—what is this?"

"This is my war team. They facilitate the movement of arms between countries. They coordinate the transfers, track the shipments, and cover our tracks when necessary." His harsh, exhaled breath made me flinch. With his chin lifted and shoulders thrown back, he surveyed the chaos on the floor.

"You operate out of a Manhattan luxury condominium

building?" My voice came out too high and thin. I cleared my throat.

"Why not? I own the building." He brushed a strand of hair behind my ear. Excitement hummed through his touch. "It's easy enough to cover up our comings and goings through the service entrances. Some of these people live here. They know how to blend."

My mind struggled to wrap around the tableau in front of me. I scanned the workers, looking for familiar faces. "It's like something out of a movie."

"But not nearly as glamorous, I can assure you."

"Are the weapons here?" I pointed to the polished concrete floor.

"No. They're stashed in warehouses across the country. I like to keep my assets spread as far apart as possible." He turned to face me, staring down into my eyes, his expression unreadable. "What are you thinking?"

"I'm not sure." Seeing the operation in action brought the situation home. If I hadn't believed it before, I believed it now. This was real. Roman had an entire secret life, one I'd never dreamed possible.

AFTER A BRIEF TOUR, WE RETURNED TO THE PENTHOUSE. While Roman showered, I paced our bedroom in anxiety-driven exhaustion. On the balcony, I contemplated our future and drank in the Manhattan skyline. A distant flash of lightning streaked across the black sky. I trembled as the wind picked up.

"You'd better come inside. It looks like a storm is blowing in." Roman's deep voice rumbled near my ear. A shiver raced down my back and settled deep inside my core. The simple sound of his voice made my heart skip a beat.

"Yes." Tiny raindrops plinked against the glass railing and splattered on my skin.

"What's going on inside that pretty head of yours?"

When I turned, he was right behind me. A snowy towel hugged his narrow waist, the edges clutched in one fist. Droplets of water fell from the ends of his rumpled hair and slid over his muscular chest. "Nothing." I bit my lower lip to suppress a gasp of surprise at his nearness.

"I didn't mean to scare you." He rubbed a hand over his bare chest and the smattering of curly black hair covering his sternum.

"You need a shave and a haircut," I said, moving away from him, putting distance between us. My fingers curled, itching with the need to rake his black locks away from his forehead. His appearance reminded me of the night I'd met him at the Masquerade de Marquis: dark, dangerous, and brimming with mystery.

"You don't like it?" He ghosted my steps, keeping us within an arm's length of each other. The scent of his shampoo and shower gel followed his movements. "I'm thinking about keeping the beard."

"No. I mean— Um— Yes. I like it. But it's just—just not your usual style." Cool, hard drywall hit my backside. I swallowed, unable to break his mesmerizing hold on my gaze.

"The barber has been the last thing on my mind lately." He ruffled a hand through his hair, sending a spray of water onto the front of my dress. The drops made small dark circles on the pale silk. We were less than six inches apart. His glance roamed over my heaving breasts before coming back to my face. "You look good in blue. Good enough to eat."

"Thanks." The solidity of my knees dissolved as he closed the remaining distance between us. From the first time we'd met, he'd had this effect on me. My nipples stung with a sudden rush of desire.

"Something's changed about you. I'm not sure what it is, but I like it." He leaned forward to brace a hand on either side of my head. The towel whispered to the floor, leaving him naked. He kicked it aside. Our body heat mingled, raising my temperature several degrees, but it was nothing compared to the fire building inside me. I'd forgotten how raw and charismatic he could be at times like these—when he wanted me. The firm line of his jaw and the rapid flutter of his pulse at the base of his throat suggested I had the same effect on him. Power flooded through me, and the sensation was more intoxicating than any drug.

"I had Christian design a new look for me." To curb the trembling of my hands, I pressed my palms against the wall beside my hips.

"Very nice. I approve, but I'm referring to something else, something inside you." His breath puffed against my ear. He punctuated his words with butterfly kisses on my ear. "And it's very, *very* sexy."

"Thank you," I said, feeling a flush creep up my neck.

"Do you know how much I love you, Rourke?" His voice lowered to a deadly whisper. We were nose to nose now, his lips close enough to send a tingle of need to my mouth. "The whole time we were apart, I thought of nothing but you and all the different ways I'd fuck you when I got you back in our bed, how I'd never again take our relationship for granted."

"Really?" I asked, unable to hold back a note of sarcasm in my voice. "Because that's not at all how it's looked."

Using his thumb and forefinger, he trapped my chin, forcing my gaze back to his. "You're always the first thing on my mind. Never doubt it." When I didn't respond, he curled one of his hands around the nape of my neck and placed the pad of his thumb on my jugular, stroking and tracing the delicate vein. My pulse thudded against his touch. Without my permission, my hips came forward, drawn by his magnetism.

His cock stood straight up, the head resting below his belly button. I moaned and closed my eyes to ease the torment building between my thighs. "You can deny our chemistry all you want, but your body is mine, Rourke. It belongs to me."

I opened my eyes and met his gaze. After we'd exchanged our wedding vows, I'd mistakenly thought the game of power had ended between us. It still existed, but the game had changed. I lifted my chin. "My body belongs to me." Temper flared in his navy irises at my denial, followed by a brief flicker of uncertainty. With my left hand, I gripped his shaft and tugged, pulling him closer to me. He grunted in surprise. "But I'm giving it to you—willingly."

"I accept." His mouth slammed against mine. Weeks of waiting and wanting had left me overheated and needy. Our dalliance at the Devil's Playground NYC had only served to fuel my lust. I whimpered and clutched his damp hair. Our tongues dueled in a battle for control. Using every inch of his torso, he pressed me to the wall. My breasts flattened against his bare chest. Through the thin fabric, the heat of his body seared my skin. When he pulled back, my chin and mouth tingled from the scrape of his beard. He fisted a hand in the hair at the nape of my neck and angled my head to the side, baring my throat to him. "I'd like to take a bite out of you. Right. Here."

"I'd like to see you try," I replied, knowing he could do anything he wanted to me, and I'd be powerless to stop him.

In one swift motion, he hoisted me to his shoulder. With my torso dangling over his back, I had a premier view of his taut, bare ass. I gave it a hard slap. He responded by dumping me on the bed. I bounced on the plush mattress, too startled to respond.

"Let's see who's in charge of whom," he said. Grabbing my ankles, he yanked my legs apart and pulled me to the edge of the bed. The hem of my dress gathered around my waist, exposing my waxed and pantyless sex to his gaze. The tip of his tongue slid over the stretch of his bottom lip. "Mrs. Menshikov, I'm shocked. Good thing I didn't know about this in the car. I would have fucked you right there, in front of Jose."

I struggled against his hold, trying to crawl backward up the bed while simultaneously tugging down my dress. In response, he flipped me onto my stomach, knocking a startled giggle out of me and shocking me with his strength. He pressed a hand into the small of my back until I quieted, then came onto the mattress with me, nudging my legs wider with his knees. I gasped at the glide of his fingers along the insides of my thighs and the occasional brush of his knuckles against my throbbing pussy. "What are you doing?"

"Surveying my kingdom," he mused, dryly. His claim made my inner walls flutter in pre-orgasmic anticipation.

"You mean, *my* kingdom." I gave an ineffective kick of my legs. "You're trespassing."

"As I recall, you gave me the keys to your kingdom a few seconds ago. *Willingly.*" His chuckle brought a flush of heat to my face. One of his fingers slipped through my wetness, teasing my entrance. I loved serious and enigmatic Roman, but I loved his playful side even more. Amid the rush of hormones and endorphins, it was hard to remember why I'd ever been angry with him. "Rourke? Are you listening?" A stinging slap on my bottom regained my attention.

"Yes." The burn of his palm print added a new layer of desire to my excitement. I vowed to let the night take its own direction. Consequences be damned.

"On your knees." He drew me onto his lap, my legs straddling him, the backs of my thighs resting on the tops of his. I leaned into the solidity of his torso. The wiry hairs of his chest tickled along my spine. Warm, strong hands cupped my breasts, thumbing the nipples, teasing me. "Better?"

"Everything is better when I'm with you." And it was true. During our time apart, I'd been half a person. Here in our bed, I remembered why. No one compared to him, to the feel of his hands on my body or the overwhelming desire he roused within me. I loved the way he challenged me and fought with me and brought excitement to my life, both emotionally and physically.

"I love you," he whispered before raining kisses along my neck and shoulders.

He spread my knees wide. Cool air brushed against my naked skin. I tried to close my legs, feeling exposed and vulnerable, then stopped myself. Needing reassurance, I turned to look at him over my shoulder. He dragged the head of his cock along my sex and pushed inside, slowly, one inch at a time. The burn and stretch of my body adjusting to his made me shudder. He smiled, and my heart melted. I lifted a hand to the back of his head and drew his mouth down to mine.

We rocked together in slow, intense rhythm. He'd never been so deep inside me before. Or so rock hard. His ragged breathing spurred my excitement. I lost myself in the slide and glide of his erection through my silky skin, desperate to scratch the itch of need that had been simmering since our estrangement. Who was I kidding? I needed him the same way I needed air to breathe. The realization made me panic. "Wait."

He froze. "Did I hurt you?"

"No." I uncoupled our bodies and turned to face him. Lines of worry etched his forehead. I smoothed them out with my fingertips. "I need to see you."

He smiled and threaded his fingers through mine before drawing my knuckles to his lips. Carefully, I lowered myself onto him. We clung to each other, his arms around my waist and mine around his neck. He nuzzled my ear. "I've shown you my worst. Are you sure you still want me?"

"It's never been about not wanting you." I took him deeper, pushing down until we were irrevocably joined. Through the open balcony doors, a police siren wailed, growing louder then dying away in the distance. "It's about whether or not we can find common ground."

"As I said, I'm open to negotiations," he said and moved me onto my back, keeping us joined. "But I have to warn you. I don't fight fair either."

CHAPTER 13
ROURKE

The next morning, I awoke to find Roman standing beside the bed, fully dressed. The loose ends of his red tie hung around his neck. He threaded his cufflinks through the holes of his sleeves, a task I'd watched him perform a hundred times before but now found overwhelmingly endearing. A lump formed in my throat. I needed to tell him about the baby. He deserved to know. I felt guilty for keeping it to myself for so long.

"Where are you going?" I asked, my voice raspy from sleep. I eased into a sitting position, waiting for signs of nausea, and exhaled in relief when my stomach remained calm.

"To work. I've got a meeting with Nicky this morning." With expert precision, he looped the tails of the tie through each other.

"Speaking of Nicky..." At the thought of his recent douchebaggery, my blood pressure began to rise. "He came by your office yesterday. He knew you were in trouble and refused to help."

Roman's brows lowered. "Really?" Blankness slid over his

face. While his expression remained neutral, a muscle ticked beneath his cheekbone. He yanked on his tie, tightening the knot. "Nicky has his own agenda, Rourke. Never forget that."

Frustration welled inside me, threatening to crack my ribs. "If he's such a problem, why don't you cut him out of your life?"

A small smile broke his mask of indifference. He smoothed his fingertips along the curve of my cheek. "Keep your friends close and your enemies closer. Have you heard that?" I nodded and leaned my face into his caress, savoring the sweetness in his touch. "Family is family. We might not be related by blood, but we grew up as brothers, and I can't disregard that connection."

Having lost my immediate family members to disease and tragedy, I understood all too well. "Can you at least control him?"

A burst of laughter shot out of him at my question. "Damn, you're a quick study."

His praised warmed my chest. I planted a kiss in the center of his palm. "I have the best as my teacher."

Catching my gaze, he sank onto the edge of the bed and smoothed my hair away from my face. "I'll be in meetings most of the day, but I'll have someone bring over my things from the hotel."

"Whoa. Hang on a second." I hoisted the sheet higher to cover my bare breasts. "I'm not sure we're ready yet."

"Didn't last night answer your questions?" He groaned and stood. With measured strides, he retrieved his jacket from its hanger on the back of the closet door. "What more do you want, Rourke?"

"I don't know." I raised my knees and wrapped my arms around my legs, miserable with uncertainty.

"I'm not a patient man."

I snorted. "That's an understatement."

He stabbed his arms into his charcoal pin-striped suit coat then yanked down his sleeves. "Now who's playing games? If you need something, just tell me, and I'll give it to you."

"I need time."

"Time for what? I've confessed my darkest sins to you, and it's still not enough. What more do you want from me?" In the act of buttoning his jacket, his elbow grazed the framed picture of us on the nightstand. It fell to the floor with a clatter. He kicked it under the bed.

"Don't yell at me." The sound of his raised voice roused my temper. I climbed to my knees and sat back on my heels, preparing for battle. "And don't be such a baby."

He growled and shook his head at the ceiling like he was praying for strength. In two strides, he was at my side and had my chin in his hand. "Listen to me. I love you. You love me. How freaking difficult is this?"

I drew in a deep breath and met his stare with equal fire. "You need to learn that you can't have everything your way all the time."

"Why not? It worked fine for me until you came along." His nostrils flared with passion.

I yanked my chin from his grasp. "Because it's not about just you anymore. It's about us. I'm pregnant." I clapped a hand over my mouth, shocked by my confession.

He backed away, running a hand through his hair and blinking like I'd slapped him. "With a baby?"

"Yes. That's usually how it happens." I rolled my eyes and immediately felt regret. In my head, I'd revealed the happy news over a candlelit dinner or in one of our quiet moments in his study. Not like this. Not in the middle of an argument.

"How long have you known?" He sank onto the edge of the bed and stared at the door.

"A few days."

"Wow." The breath left his lungs in a startled whoosh. I

curled my fingers into fists and waited for his stunned expression to fade. "Are you sure?" His voice cracked.

"I haven't had a formal test yet, but yes. I'm sure. You're going to be a dad again."

His phone buzzed on the nightstand. He silenced it, his movements slow and controlled. When he lifted his eyes to mine, happiness filled their depths. A smile curled his mouth. "That's fantastic."

"Under different circumstances, I'd be thrilled, but not now. The timing couldn't be worse."

"It's never an ideal time. We'll make it work." He wrapped his arms around me and dragged me to his chest. His chin rested on the top of my head. After a few heartbeats, he placed a hand on my tummy. "I can't wait to have this baby with you. You've made me the happiest man on the planet." His embraced tightened.

I inhaled his clean scent, burying my nose in the nook beneath his ear. "Really?" A surge of hormones sent me to the edge of tears. I dug my fingers into his back, holding him close. "Because I'm scared for our future, Roman. I can't raise a child in this kind of craziness." Once my emotions had calmed, I said, "I need security."

"I'll make it happen. I promise." He lowered his face to the curve of my neck and squeezed me. "This changes everything for us." His phone buzzed again. With a reluctant sigh, he pulled away. "That's Spitz. I have to go. We'll talk about this tonight, okay?"

CHAPTER 14
ROMAN

S pitz was waiting for me when I reached the lobby. He joined me in the back of the Maybach so we could discuss my current situation. Rourke's refusal to let me come home and the announcement of her pregnancy spurred me to act. I understood her misgivings and vowed to obliterate them. Her acceptance became my ultimate prize.

"I want to know who's behind this bullshit, Spitz. No more playing around. Get me names. Whoever it is, they're fucking with the wrong man."

A grin brightened his normally somber face. "About damn time. Glad to have you back, boss."

"Don't thank me quite yet. You're going to earn every penny of that outrageous salary I pay you." I thumbed through the emails on my tablet. Without Rourke's assistance, I'd fallen behind in my correspondence.

"I've already put a tail on a few persons of interest. I'll have a full report for you tomorrow."

"And do a security assessment on the penthouse. I want estimates for the necessary upgrades or modifications. Spare no expense."

"Got it." His fingers moved rapidly as he typed notes into his phone.

"I want state-of-the-art. No second-rate bullshit." A dozen new emails pinged into my inbox. I sighed. For someone like me, work never ended. "And watch Nicky, would you? Make sure he's not going rogue." In the past, I'd found my brother's competitive nature amusing, but not anymore. I had to wonder how far he'd go in his attempts to undermine my relationship with Rourke.

"You want me to talk to him?"

"No, I'll deal with him." I tapped out a quick text to Nicky, reminding him of our meeting at my hotel room.

Two hours later, he stood in front of the fireplace of my suite, eyes bloodshot and scowling. "You rang, Your Majesty?"

"You're late."

"Not everyone gets up at an ungodly hour like you." He stalked to the liquor cabinet. The sounds of clinking glass and flowing liquid filled the silence between us as he poured two fingers of Glenlivet over ice.

"It's a little early for that, isn't it?"

"For you, it's early. For me, it's late. I haven't been home yet. As soon as you're done berating me, I'm going to bed." He closed his eyes and nosed the scotch. "Ah. Pear, orange, black cherry. Single malt. A hint of oak. No one distills like the Scots."

"Agreed." I set my laptop on the coffee table and rested my elbows on my knees to study him. Despite his claims of being out all night, his suit was unwrinkled, his hair perfect. "But I didn't bring you here to discuss liquor."

"What have I done wrong this time?" He returned to the window and stared down at the street.

"Stop running your mouth to Rourke."

He snorted. "I didn't tell her anything she shouldn't already know." I winced at the truth in his statement. My refusal to communicate with her had led to us sleeping in separate beds. He tapped a fingernail against the rim of the glass. "If you're going to drag her into your underworld, she needs to understand the dangers."

"Rourke will be fine as long as you keep your nose out of my business." I mimicked his stance at the other window to contemplate his words. From this position, I could see Central Park and the splashing waters of the Pulitzer Fountain in Grand Army Plaza. What if Nicky was right? I wanted to spoil Rourke and give her all the luxuries my money could afford, but perhaps I'd been naive. More and more, my business world overlapped with my personal life. It was one of the reasons I'd avoided serious relationships in the past.

"Are you done? I'm starting to lose my second wind," he said after a heavy sigh.

"No. One more thing." I kept my voice level and quiet. "I asked you to use your relationship with Everly to dig up dirt on McElroy. I didn't mean for you to fuck her and dump her."

He scrubbed a hand over his face. "Well, maybe you'll be more explicit next time."

"If you don't get your shit together, there won't be a next time. I'm starting to doubt your commitment to our cause. I can't spend time worrying about you when there are real issues needing my attention."

"What's that supposed to mean?"

"It means I'm done catering to your immaturity. I don't have the time or interest."

"Am I out? Is that what you're saying?" Alarm flashed in his eyes.

"I'm saying I'm not sure I can trust you anymore." I returned to the sofa and rested an ankle on top of my knee, stretching my arms across the back.

"Don't be ridiculous. I'm your brother."

"You're a liability. You've defied me at every turn. First

with Claudette and Milada. Now with Rourke. I've turned a blind eye to your shenanigans because you're family, but I've got too much at stake now. Man up, Nicky. We're under siege. Either you're with me, or you're against me."

"That's bullshit, and you know it." The heels of his Italian shoes thudded softly on the hardwood floor as he paced in front of the fireplace.

"Actions speak louder than words, and your actions show a decided disrespect for everything we've done to date." I shrugged. "There's no reason for us to part as enemies. I've had my legal team draw up papers of separation for our joint businesses." I pushed documents across the coffee table toward him. "I think you'll find the terms more than generous. Those are your copies. You can take them with you. Have your attorney look them over."

"You're fucking kidding me." He stared at me in disbelief.

"We both know I never kid about business." I nudged the papers forward another inch. "Don't worry. You can still come over for Christmas dinner."

"I don't give a fuck about Christmas dinner." He raked both of his hands through his hair, frazzling the ends into disarray. "You'd seriously cut me out like this?"

"I'll do what I have to do to keep my family and business safe."

"*I'm* your family." Judging by the panic on his face, I'd hit his most vulnerable spot. More than anything, Nicky feared being penniless and alone. He sagged onto the sofa across from me, shoulders lowering in defeat. "Fine. No more shenanigans. Just don't cut me out."

"We have an understand?"

He nodded.

"Great." I glanced at my watch. "I've got a conference call. Let me know when you've got something on McElroy."

The door thudded closed behind him. I gathered the

documents he'd left behind and dropped them in the shredder. They were copies of a proposal for one of my projects. Good thing he hadn't called my bluff.

☙❧

THE REST OF THE DAY PASSED QUICKLY. I MISSED LUNCH, too absorbed in work, forcing my thoughts to stay focused on the business I'd been neglecting. The sun had lowered in the sky when Lorissa buzzed into my office.

"Sir, Mrs. Menshikov is on the phone. She says it's urgent."

Rourke hadn't called me once since we'd returned from England. After the tumultuous start to our day, I wasn't sure what to think. I'd been expecting one of my German business partners for a conference call instead. Unease knotted my stomach. "Put her through."

"Roman, they're tearing the entire place apart." Panic lifted her voice to a higher pitch.

"Who? What are you talking about?" My elbow grazed the coffee cup on the corner of the desk. The porcelain mug plummeted to the floor, shattering into a dozen pieces.

"The police are here with a warrant." Her breath puffed against the phone.

"Hold tight. I'm on my way."

☙❧

ONE OF THE BENEFITS OF BEING WEALTHY WAS HAVING A room full of lawyers at your disposal. I grabbed John Hardin, one of the senior corporate attorneys, a man whose integrity I trusted, and bundled him into the waiting car. On the drive to the penthouse, I called Spitz and asked him to meet us there.

Hardin ran a finger around the inside of his shirt collar as the car paused at the front entrance to the building. "I haven't practiced criminal law in twenty years. I'm not sure how much help I'll be, but I'll do what I can."

A scruffy-looking agent in an expensive suit and cheap shoes met us when we stepped out of the elevator. He flashed his badge, a shit-eating grin on his face. "Mr. Menshikov, I'm Agent Frankel. We're here for evidence connected to the murder of Lavender Cunningham."

"This is my attorney, John Hardin. You can deal with him." I nodded to John, ignoring Frankel's outstretched hand. "Where's my wife?"

Rourke sat on the sofa in the living room with her arms hugging her waist. The worry on her face punched me in the gut. I'd done this to her.

I shoved past him and raced to her side. "Are you okay?"

"I'm fine, but this is crazy." She buried her face in my shoulder, small and frightened in my embrace. "I've been out all day running errands and came back to this—this chaos. I'm so sorry, Roman. I'd never have let them in if I'd been here."

"It's not your fault." I pressed a kiss to the top of her head. "Don't worry. Let them search. They won't find anything." The tenseness in her shoulders eased. I tipped her face up to mine. "I'm going to go talk to Hardin and see what's going on."

"I'm not an expert, but the warrant seems legit," Hardin said, scanning over the document.

"Absolutely everything is in order, Mr. Menshikov." From the very first, I hated Frankel's smug, asinine grin.

"If you want to waste your time, go ahead. I have nothing to hide." I shrugged nonchalantly, but my insides seethed with fury. "But you'd better damn well be sure you've covered all your bases, because I'll have your job for this."

He snickered. "I doubt that."

Meanwhile, a pair of men carried my desktop computer into the elevator. Unfortunately for him, the entire unit had been replaced twenty-four hours earlier and harbored nothing but basic software.

"Really?" I cocked an eyebrow. "I bet the Bureau doesn't know about your love for the ponies and whores, for that matter. What about your eight-year-old daughter? Does she know? Angelica, right?"

The color drained from his face. Spitz had used his connections to dig up the dirty laundry of every agent on Lavender's case. Thank goodness I'd taken the time to study the information. "Are you threatening me, Mr. Menshikov?" His features pulled downward in a scowl. "Because we can take this discussion down to the station, if necessary."

"Did you hear a threat in that, Hardin?" I asked.

"No, sir, I didn't." He stepped to my side. "However, your continued hounding of Mr. Menshikov is clearly harassment. If you have evidence, then you need to charge him."

"No need to get your panties in a twist, Mr. Hardin. We're done here." Frankel's flat stare met mine. "We'll meet again soon, Mr. Menshikov. I can promise you that."

The elevator doors closed behind Frankel and the last of his men.

Spitz burst into the room ten seconds later from the penthouse service entrance, red-faced and breathless. "Sorry I'm late."

"About fucking time," I growled. "Can you explain what just happened?"

"I haven't had time to check yet, but I can assure you, this won't happen again."

"Find out who let them in this apartment and fire their ass. No one should ever get through the door without my approval. This is inexcusable." Now that Frankel had left, my temper reached the boiling point. "I pay your security team big bucks. A breach like this is a fucking travesty."

"I agree." His face hardened, the lines above his forehead deepening. "I'll take care of it."

"My daughter works for the District Attorney. Let me make some calls and see what I can find out," John said.

"Thanks. I appreciate that." I clapped him on the shoulder.

Rourke rose from the sofa, her blue eyes round and solemn, and crossed the room to join us, picking her way through the debris left in the wake of the search. I put an arm around her waist, tucking her into my side. She pushed away. "It's going to take forever to clean this up."

"Let's go back to my hotel. Our staff can take care of it." I expected her to object, but after a second glance around the room, she nodded.

In that moment, I vowed to take my revenge on every single person who'd brought this witch hunt into fruition. No one fucked with me, and no one ever fucked with my wife.

CHAPTER 15
ROURKE

That evening, with the patter of rain on the hotel windows, Roman and I laid side by side beneath the soft sheets of The Plaza bed. The physical pull between us refused to be ignored, and sex provided a distraction from the trauma of the day. When I closed my eyes and rested my nose below his ear, it was easy to forget the chaos of the outside world, if only for a few hours.

His leg brushed against mine, his hairy thigh sending gooseflesh along my skin. The strength had ebbed from my body, leaving me boneless and sated after our marathon of fucking. He turned on his side to face me, propping his head on an elbow, and watched me with hooded eyes. The tips of his fingers trailed from my sternum to my navel, back and forth. We didn't speak for a long time, just stared at each other. A crack of thunder reverberated through the walls, sending me deeper into his arms.

"How are you feeling?" he asked, breaking the silence.

"Fine."

"Have you had any morning sickness?"

"A little, but not bad. Certain smells seem to set me off. If

I can make it through breakfast, I'm okay." I lifted a hand to ward off this line of questioning. "Don't jinx me."

"I want to go to the doctor with you. Be sure to put your appointments on my calendar." His hand came to a stop on my lower belly.

"If I was still your assistant, I would," I said, baiting him.

"Are you starting trouble already?"

"Nope. Just stating a fact."

Amusement curved his lips. "I'm never going to be able to control you, am I?"

"And yet, you keep trying." Despite my best efforts, I couldn't evade rolling my eyes.

"Well, I wouldn't have you any other way." He pressed a kiss to my belly then rested his chin on my chest, blinking up at me.

"Sometimes, I think you're more manipulative than Nicky. Just because I can't keep my hands off you doesn't mean you're going to get out of talking." I ran my hand through his hair. Quiet moments like this meant more to me than any amount of money, but reality beckoned.

"Where do you want to start?" He began tracing figure-eights around my navel.

I sucked in a deep breath and gathered my courage. "Was Lavender part of the Russian mafia?"

Roman's finger stopped. He shifted into a sitting position, rested his elbows on his uplifted knees, and stared past the end of the bed at the thunderous sky. "It depends on what you mean by 'mafia.' They're more like hostile allies."

An unsettling thought made my stomach twist. "Are *you* part of this mafia?"

"Hell no. I don't have time for that shit. That's Nicky's game." He cast a mischievous grin in my direction. "We do rub shoulders from time to time. My adoptive father was affiliated, but my allegiance lies elsewhere."

"Right." I nodded and tried to look away, wanting to hide an inexplicable sting of tears. I swiped at my eyes. "I don't know what's wrong with me. I'm not even sad."

"You've got a ton of hormones raging in your body right now, and you've gone through quite a shock. Give yourself a break. Too much worry is bad for you and the baby." The darkness in his eyes softened. "We've got a chance to build a new family." Warmth spread through my insides as he rested his hand on my stomach. "There's nothing I wouldn't do for you. You know that, right?"

"Yes." Despite the many challenges and betrayals in his history, he remained loyal to those around him. Being alone in bed without the pressures of work or war to pull us apart, encompassed by his love, gave me hope.

He tilted his head to one side, studying my eyes. "I get why you're concerned. I haven't done a very good job of making you feel secure, but you're safe with me, Rourke. I have the money and resources to protect us. I'll build a damn fortress for us, if that's what it takes."

I took his hand in mine and nestled my cheek into his palm. "I promised to love you forever, Roman. I meant every word of it. Although, your actions today didn't help your cause."

The line of his lips curved into a smile. "Nothing matters more to me than you."

"I need honesty and trust and for you to show a little confidence in my ability to be at your side."

"You're my queen, Rourke Menshikov. If you weren't worthy, I wouldn't have married you." He leaned in to give me a kiss.

"And you're my king." I closed my eyes, savoring the softness of his lips and the gentle intrusion of his tongue. My heartbeats scattered, buoyed on a rush of desire.

From the dresser, his phone buzzed insistently. He pulled

away, eyes dark with lust, and scrubbed a hand over his face. He crossed the room, naked, not bothering with his robe. "It might be Spitz. I should take it."

"It's okay. Go ahead." I hoisted the bedsheet higher, tucked it beneath my armpits, and sat up, wincing at the multitude of aches in my thoroughly sexed-up body.

"It's not okay." He swiped the phone screen with the pad of his thumb, instantly shifting into mogul mode. "Spitz, you'd better have a good fucking reason for interrupting my evening." I swung my legs over the edge of the bed, preparing to get dressed. He pointed a finger at me. "You. Don't move. I'm not done with you yet."

Heat and pleasure warmed my face. I smiled, settled back against the headboard, and let the sheet sag suggestively to reveal my breasts. He shook his head. In return, I tweaked one of my nipples, pulling and tugging it into a tight point. His cock twitched and lengthened. He dropped a hand to stroke it. I lifted an eyebrow and patted the empty mattress at my side.

"Are you sure about that?" he asked Spitz. The smile fell from his lips. He shoved a hand through his hair and began to pace. "Don't tell me this unless you're absolutely, one-hundred-percent certain. I want proof."

I admired his muscular body, the width of his shoulders, and the way his torso tapered down to a rock-hard ass. Dark, wiry hair dusted his thighs and calves. His dick stood at attention, bobbing up and down with each stride. I sucked in a breath, overwhelmed by the sight of him, knowing this dangerous man belonged to me.

He ended the call and tossed the phone on the bed. "Get dressed. Spitz needs a meeting."

"Now?" I scrambled to my feet, taking the sheet with me.

"You said you want to be included." His palm landed on my bottom with a playful smack.

"A little notice would've been nice." I shuffled through my suitcase for a pair of jeans and a T-shirt. Roman plucked the sheet from around my shoulders and tossed it to the floor. I rolled my eyes at him. "Not helping, Mr. Menshikov."

"You just don't appreciate my talents." His eyes darkened as they roamed over my naked figure. I stepped into a pair of panties then pushed my arms through the straps of a matching bra. He placed a hand on each of my shoulders, turned me to face the wall, and fastened the hooks in the back. His warm hands smoothed along my ribs and ended at my hips. "Dressing you is almost—but not quite—as much fun as stripping you down."

I flashed a smile over my shoulder at him. "Spitz is waiting. Remember?"

"How could I forget?"

"You know, he doesn't have a very high opinion of me."

"Why do you say that?" His lips tickled along the curve of my shoulder.

"He's made a few comments here and there." I bit my lower lip, wondering how to proceed.

His kisses stopped at my collarbone. "What did he say?" I pulled a sweater over my head and headed for the bathroom to brush my teeth. Roman's hand wrapped around my elbow to stop my escape. "Rourke, tell me."

"He doesn't like me much." Our eyes met. I glanced down to escape his penetrating gaze. "He doesn't like me much."

"You're bothered by it, or you wouldn't have brought it up." He rested a hip on the edge of the bathroom vanity to study my reflection in the mirror. A muscle ticked beneath his cheekbone. Guilt lessened some of the animosity I felt toward Spitz. Roman had more problems than he could handle right now. He didn't need my insecurities added to his list.

"Just forget I said anything. I don't care if he likes me or not, as long as you do." To soften his mood, I dropped a kiss on the end of his nose. "I probably overreacted."

"I'll talk to him." His eyebrows lowered. "No one disrespects my wife. Ever. He's a damn genius at his job, but I'll fire him, if you want."

"No. Don't worry about it." I lifted my chin and gave him a bright smile. "I'll take care of it. If I'm going to be a war king's wife, I'd better start acting like one."

He watched in silence as I brushed my teeth. I rinsed my mouth and turned to face him. With a few quick twists, I coiled my frazzled hair into a bun. His gaze roamed over me. One corner of his mouth twitched, like he was holding back a smile. "What?" I glanced down at the fly of my jeans to make sure it was zipped.

"You never cease to amaze me." Pride gleamed in his eyes. "Get over here."

I wrapped my arms around his neck. He pulled me between his knees and slipped his hands into my back pockets. Every time he held me, I melted. No matter how long we were married, I'd never grow tired of his touch. I rested my head on his shoulder. We stood there for a minute, savoring the novelty of being together after such a long separation. With a groan, he eased me back a step. "I'm going to need more of this later, but right now, we need to take care of business.

"Okay." I had no idea what Spitz was about to say, but I didn't care as long as Roman stood beside me. He clasped his hand around mine. We walked to the door together.

At the threshold, he paused and gave me a quick, light kiss. "Buckle up, Mrs. Menshikov. You're in for a bumpy ride."

CHAPTER 16
ROURKE

Fifteen minutes later, I sat on the edge of a chair in Roman's hotel study. The space between my legs throbbed to the point of distraction. Earlier, Roman had banged me against the shower wall with so much force and fervor that I'd thought the tile might crack. Now he sat behind his hotel desk, staring at his laptop, cool and reserved in a white polo shirt and dark jeans.

"Hey, boss." Spitz knocked on the open door and entered the room. His gaze hit mine and flicked away. "Good evening, Mrs. Menshikov. I apologize for the inconvenience." Although his words were polite, his lack of eye contact and flat tone suggested otherwise.

I lifted my chin and glanced at Roman. He drummed his fingers on the desk and stared at me. "If you need privacy, I can go to the kitchen. I'm starving." Knowing Roman, his hotel room had been fully stocked with groceries and snacks.

"You're staying." Roman's voice held a note of warning.

"He doesn't want me here."

"It's not his decision." Challenge flashed in Roman's gaze. "It's yours and mine." His show of faith bolstered my confidence. He was handing me the opportunity to stand up for my rights as his wife.

I nodded. "I'll stay."

Spitz opened his mouth to speak, but Roman cut him off. "Unless you're about to agree with me, this subject is closed."

"Whatever you want is good with me." Spitz lifted both palms into the air and claimed the chair to my right. His weary sigh contradicted his agreement. "Time is wasting and I'm eager to get to work." Judging from the redness of his eyes and the scruff on his jaw, he hadn't slept much over the past few days.

"You look like shit," Roman said, iterating my thoughts. He put his computer to sleep and swiveled the chair to face us.

"Shit would be an improvement," Spitz mused. "How about you? How's that gunshot wound healing?"

"Fine." In response, he touched his side. "What have you got for us?"

"Photos from a surveillance camera at the back entrance of Ms. Cunningham's apartment." As he spoke, he pulled a large envelope from his briefcase. He spread a series of grainy black-and-white photos on the desk. I leaned forward for a better view. He tapped the center photo. "There's your problem."

Roman groaned and shifted back in his chair, spreading his knees wide and swiping both palms over his face. "Are you fucking kidding me with this?"

"What? Who is it?" I squinted and grabbed the nearest picture. My guts twisted.

"When was this taken?" Roman asked.

"The day she died," Spitz said, watching my expression carefully.

I pressed a hand to my mouth, hoping to hold back the rise of bile. There was no mistaking the face of the man standing next to a white limousine. Mr. McElroy had his hand Lavender Cunningham's back, his touch unmistakably intimate, as they prepared to enter the car. As if this revelation wasn't devastating enough, the third person in the photo was Everly.

I REFUSED TO BELIEVE MY EYES. THE PHOTOGRAPH psychologically burned my fingers. I dropped it onto the desk and wiped my hands on my thighs to clear away the sensation of uncleanliness. Roman continued rifling through the pictures. He landed on one of the couple kissing while Everly looked away. The Everly I knew would never condone this kind of behavior from her father. Not after the way her husband had cheated on her. Yet, there she was, standing beside the former Vice President and his mistress.

"There's more." Spitz thumbed through the notes in his phone. "I have reason to believe former Vice President McElroy has been following you, Mrs. Menshikov, since you had dinner at his house. He's had two men on your tail. And, according to Lavender's doorman, he's been visiting Ms. Cunningham in the middle of the night for over two years."

My mind raced to make the connections. "Maybe he's a cheater, but I can't believe he had anything to do with her death." Mr. McElroy's betrayal of his wife hurt me almost as much as if he were my own father. I lifted one of the photos for a closer look. Everly's mouth was drawn down into a scowl. Not the expression of a happy camper. I stared into her eyes, desperate to decipher her expression, desperate for clues about her state of mind. This scenario directly contradicted our pact to remove secrets from our relationship. She'd never lied to me about something so big.

"His name kept cropping up on the streets. Nothing

major. Just small mentions here and there." Spitz slumped back in his chair. The leather creaked at the shift in his weight. He closed his eyes and swallowed, his Adam's apple bobbing up and down. "At first, I thought it was an unlucky coincidence. I made a few calls to my friends and found out he's been playing both sides of the political field since before he took office."

"Wouldn't the FBI have checked this camera in their investigation?" I asked, unable to accept the validity of the photograph.

"Absolutely. In fact, they seized the original footage. Lucky for us, the security guy always makes a backup and has a fondness for Benjamin Franklin." Spitz lifted an eyebrow, still avoiding my gaze. His direct refusal to make eye contact made my blood simmer. What the hell had made him so hostile?

Roman grimaced and massaged his forehead with two fingers. "This is all very interesting, but I want concrete proof of his connection. What else have you got? "

"My source says that McElroy has been diverting funds to the rebels who overthrew your father, and he intends to do the same with Androvia." He withdrew several sheets of paper from the envelope and slid them toward Roman. "Here's a copy his personal emails. For a high-level politician, he doesn't have very good firewalls."

"You hacked into the former Vice President's email?" My mouth dropped open at his audacity.

"Technically, no. I hired someone to do it." He directed his answer to Roman. "Anyway, it's all there. Dates, times, places, and the order to have suspicion thrown to you over Lavender's death."

"This can't be right," I whispered, more to myself than anyone else.

"It might be wise for you to keep contact with Ms.

McElroy to a minimum until we've resolved her involvement in this issue," Spitz said.

"She's my best friend." My feelings of dislike toward him exploded. "No way."

Roman thumbed through the emails then blew out a loud sigh. His gaze lifted to meet mine. "I'm sorry, princess. He's got a point. Avoiding all the McElroys is mandatory. Mr. McElroy in particular."

In my mind, the McElroys represented everything good about my past. Memories came flooding back. Vacations spent at their summer home. My five-year-old self being carried up to Everly's bedroom in Mr. McElroy's strong arms when we fell asleep in front of the TV. The way they'd supported me after my parents' funeral. Tears stung my eyes. If I couldn't trust them, how could I trust anyone?

"Baby?" Roman's voice cut through the chaos in my head. I blinked up at him. In one swift movement, he was beside me. He pushed the hair back from face and tilted my head to stare into my eyes. "Are you okay?"

"No." My voice wavered. I'd never be okay again, but this wasn't the time for a breakdown. "It's like hearing that Santa Claus and the Easter Bunny aren't real—all on the same day. I'm just...just really disappointed." I sat up straighter and lifted my chin, giving him a small smile. Brooding wouldn't help anyone. I needed to compartmentalize, and fast. "I'll deal with it. Go on."

"Someone with internal access is giving up vital information about you, boss. I'm going to run checks on all the house and security staff."

"Of course. Do whatever you need." Roman shifted. His bare forearm skimmed across mine, sending a ripple of desire up my arm.

I swallowed down guilt. How could I feel pleasure and be so devastated at the same time?

An awkward silence stretched through the room. Spitz pinched his lips together, a furrow spreading across his brow. Roman studied him for a minute then smiled in a way that made my panties dampen. He threaded his fingers through mine.

"Can I have a moment alone with you, sir?" Spitz asked. "It's personal."

"No problem." I gave both men a smile. When I caught Roman's eyes, I saw puzzlement in their depths. "I'm still thinking about raiding the kitchen. Can I get anything for either of you?" Although my nerves were frazzled, my belly growled, broadcasting its emptiness to the room. I stood.

Roman, still holding my hand, pulled me down until my lips leveled with his. "A kiss before you go, please."

I closed my eyes and savored the press of his mouth against mine, the taste of peppermint, and the scent of his shampoo.

He tilted his head back and gazed down at me. "Whipped cream."

"What?" I lifted my eyebrows, confused.

"I'm ready for dessert. Take it to our bedroom. Don't start without me." There was no mistaking the wickedness in his tone.

Embarrassment heated my face. I closed the door behind me and paused outside the room. The tension between me and Spitz had been unbearable. Uneasiness lifted the fine hairs on the back of my neck. I had a feeling his "personal business" had something to do with me.

CHAPTER 17

ROMAN

Before leaving, Rourke stopped at the study door and cast a questioning glance over her shoulder. God, she was beautiful. Her creamy skin glowed with good health. The loose ends of her blond hair fluttered around her shoulders. Later, I was going to wrap those silky strands around my dick. I lifted an eyebrow, daring her to question my request for whipped cream. Instead of giving me sass, she broke into a wide smile, the first one of the day. My pulse skittered. I'd trade every dollar in my possession to keep that smile on her face for the rest of her life. If it meant giving up my secret life, I'd do it. Our connected gazes strengthened the pull between us. My self-control wavered. I shoved back my chair, ready to follow her.

Vaguely, from far away, Spitz's voice droned. "Boss?" His tone held a note of annoyance.

"What?" The leather chair creaked as I shifted. Whatever personal business he needed to address had better be quick and to the point.

He leaned forward, resting his elbows on his thighs and

clasping his hands between his knees. His gaze found the floor and stayed there. "I'm not sure how to say this."

"Just say it." My patience, already stretched thin by sexual desire and lack of sleep, snapped.

"How much do you trust your wife?"

"Are you fucking kidding me with this?" I shoved away from the desk, ready to throttle him. "We've already had this discussion one too many times."

"Hear me out." He lifted a hand and leaned back.

"You'd better explain yourself. Right the fuck now." No one disrespected Rourke. As much as I esteemed Spitz, our partnership ended at my wife's feet.

"Someone within your organization is leaking information. I'd be remiss if I didn't look at every single person. The way I see it, she's got means, motive, and opportunity." He ticked off the points with his fingers. "Means—she has intimate access to your contacts, schedules, and private information. She's close friends with your biggest enemy and his daughter. Motive—if you're out of the picture, she gains control of your estate and becomes an obscenely wealthy woman. Opportunity—she's alone in your office and penthouse. You don't know what she's doing in her free time. Not to mention her recent behavior. After you were taken into custody, she spent the time buying ball gowns and attended a dinner party at the McElroy house. Not exactly the actions of a heartbroken wife."

Although I didn't want to give credence to his theory, he had solid facts. On paper, Rourke appeared to be a leading suspect. In my heart, however, I knew better. No matter how angry or upset she might be, she'd never betray me. I shook my head. "You need to look elsewhere. You're wasting your time with her when you could be investigating the real culprit."

"You've got to admit, it's possible." Ignoring my protests,

he continued. "She came back to New York, knowing you'd follow her here, knowing the danger you'd be in. She knows your deepest, darkest secrets. If anyone could breach your security, this girl could do it. Do you really think her introduction into your life was by accident? Think about. Ivan told me how she crashed your masquerade without an invitation at the urging of Everly McElroy. It's almost too perfect."

I drummed my fingertips on the desk and weighed his words. He stared back, challenging me in a way few people had the balls to do. His accusations made sense. I stood, walked to the door, and opened it. "We're done here." Despite my cool tone, my guts churned.

To his credit, he changed track, his features impassive. "If you're convinced she's not involved, I'll respect your opinion." He smoothed his trousers down his legs with his palms as he straightened. "Where do you want me to begin?"

"Lavender is the obvious choice."

"I'll work backward from her and see if I can find any connections with your staff."

"Great."

At the threshold, he paused and met my gaze. "Your wife to watch herself around Ms. McElroy. We don't know her place in all this. And I don't think Mrs. Menshikov appreciates the seriousness of your predicament."

"Let me worry about Rourke and Everly." My words were confident, but inside, I was shaken to the core. Was I so blinded by my love for her that I couldn't see the truth? My father's faith in his friends had led to the murders of my entire immediate family. I had no intention of following in his footsteps.

As I returned to the master suite, snippets of long-forgotten information resurfaced in my head. What if Rourke had been planted by McElroy? I had no way to verify the truth except to ask her. A question like that would rock our shaky marriage to its foundation. When I opened the bedroom door, Rourke's head jerked up, and a flush climbed into her face. She was sitting cross-legged in the center of the bed with her phone in her lap, fingers tapping relentlessly as she texted. A silver serving tray held a bowl of potato chips, a container of chocolate mousse, and an aerosol can of whipped cream. I sat beside her and tucked a loose lock of her hair behind her ear.

"You'd better not be working." I strained to get a look at the screen then felt immediate shame for doubting her.

"No. Of course not." She closed the text message screen, but not before Everly's name flashed in the message box. The color heightened in her cheeks.

"You look guilty. Are you disobeying my orders?" I waited for her to confess, my unease growing.

"The only thing I'm guilty of is thinking dirty thoughts about you." Her laughter sounded unnatural. She leaned forward and placed a kiss on the notch of my collarbone. The muscles in my groin tightened.

"Is that so?" I angled my chin to allow her better access. Although her kisses sizzled across my skin, my stomach churned. Spitz's accusations had made me paranoid.

"Yep." She shifted to straddle my lap, but I couldn't staunch the doubts in my head. "I've got plans for you, mister."

"Hold that thought." I eased her to the mattress and headed toward the bathroom. I needed a minute to pull myself together. With hands braced on the sink, I stared at my reflection. What was wrong with me? I looked the same on the outside but felt completely different inside. A few hours ago, I'd been confident—cocky, even—about our future. Spitz's accusations had rocked me to the core.

I splashed water on my face and headed back to my wife. As I reached for a hand towel, a scrap of paper caught my eye. It was on the tile floor beneath Rourke's bathrobe, like it had fallen from her pocket. I scooped it up and unfolded it. Prince Heinrich's name and number were written on a message form from the office. A dull ache thudded behind my eyes. Why in God's name would Rourke have Prince Heinrich's personal cell phone number?

"If you don't get out here, I'm going to start without you," Rourke called from the other side of the door.

Was she a spy? The thought of her duplicity hurt more than my healing gunshot wound. I was Roman Menshikov. No one defied me. *Ever.* I crumpled the paper in my fist and stormed from the room.

When I caught sight of her, the breath whooshed from my lungs. She was lying on her stomach in the center of the bed, legs waving in the air behind her, completely nude. In the soft light of the nightstand lamps, her skin shimmered like satin. I swallowed hard around the tightness in my throat, willing my temper into submission. This wasn't the time to be irrational. She rolled onto her back and stretched, her movements slow and languid, and blinked up at me with round doe eyes. "Good Lord," I muttered to myself.

A mischievous grin bowed her mouth. "You took forever. Come and join me." She patted the empty mattress at her side. "I'm so lonely." The movement jiggled her breasts.

I licked my lips at the sight of her nipples, tight and pink, pointing toward the ceiling.

My second brain, the one inside my pants, warred for control. He couldn't wait to sink himself inside her. I yanked my shirt over my head and placed a knee on the bed, intending to fuck the truth out of her. She inched backward on the mattress, mirroring my movements.

I wrapped a hand around her throat, pushing her into a position of submission. "Spread your legs for me." She hesitated, but not from fear. I'd seen that look in her eyes before

—a combination of rebellion and excitement. "Do it," I commanded.

"So bossy." She lifted her chin a notch.

I shoved a knee between her thighs and opened them wide. A startled squeak escaped her lips. The flush of arousal crept up her chest, over her breasts, and to her collarbone. She loved playing the victim as much as I loved playing the villain. Her compliance hardened my dick to the point of pain. I needed to be inside her. Immediately.

The tip of her tongue swept over her bottom lip. "Come on, Roman. What are you waiting for? Fuck me."

"Sit tight, pretty girl. I'm about to deliver on that request." Nothing excited me more than a dirty mouth on a sweet-looking female. *Correction*—nothing excited me more than Rourke's dirty mouth. She rarely cursed in front of me, but when she did, I felt an immediate response in my groin. Shifting my weight to an elbow and retaining my grip on her throat, I slammed into her. No foreplay. No bullshit. The force of my movements shoved her up the bed.

"Ahhhhh." Her moan fired up the animal inside me. I drove through her slickness, taking my pleasure from her, demanding her submission.

"Do you love me?" I asked.

"Yes." She lifted her knees and wrapped her legs around my waist.

I kept pounding, like I could somehow force a confession out of her. "And you would never betray me?"

Her eyes, which had closed, flew open. I tightened my fingers on the column of her neck. "No. Never." Every stroke of my cock made her grunt.

As I gazed down on her loveliness, a rush of tenderness swept through me. The thing was, for once in my life, I had no desire to manipulate this person. I wanted her to be with me because she loved me. No other reason. "Why?" Our bodies slapped together. The harsh smack of flesh on flesh filled the quiet room. "Why do you love me?"

"Because—because you're—the one." She lifted her arms and braced them against the headboard to keep the top of her head from crashing into it. "The only one, Roman."

I slipped a hand between us and found her clit with my middle finger. She hissed at the contact. Moving swiftly, relentlessly, I stroked her hard and fast. "Look at me when you come."

The walls of her pussy fluttered then clenched hard around me. Her shoulders came off the bed with the force of her orgasm, but she kept her gaze locked with mine. "Yes. Oh, God. Oh, yes." Her pupils dilated, overtaking the blue of her irises.

Pride swelled inside me, knowing I could bring her to climax so quickly. "Don't move. I want to come on your tits." Seeing her excitement, feeling her tight walls around my cock, brought me to the edge of sanity. The burn of release raced down my legs. She felt too damn good. It was a wonder I'd held my orgasm this long. I pumped into her twice then pulled out. My cock, swollen and covered in her slickness, bobbed on her chest. I threw my head back and roared at the satisfaction as I spurted on her breasts, marking her as mine.

Slowly, the rush of fulfillment ebbed away and left me with nothing but shame. "Jesus. Fuck." I sat back on my knees and shoved both hands through my hair.

"What? What's wrong?" She lifted to her elbows, her eyes wide.

"I'm sorry." Red fingerprints blotched the white skin of her neck. *My* fingerprints. I was an animal—a beast. I'd never lost control with her before, not like this. "I don't know what came over me."

"Roman, it's okay." She climbed to her knees and took my face between her palms. I tried to avoid her eyes. "It was—"

A blush crept into her cheeks. "No one has ever— I mean, this is the first time— I had no idea that sort of thing would turn me on so much."

"But your neck." I couldn't look at the evidence of my disgrace. Instead, I tore away from her grasp and stared out the window.

"Stop." She gently turned my face back to her and placed a fingertip on my lips. "You didn't hurt me at all. I loved every minute of it."

"I'm so fucked up. I don't know who I can trust anymore."

"You can always trust me, Roman." The edge of her teeth worried the plumpness of her bottom lip. "What brought this on?"

I wrapped one of the sheets around her shoulders. She leaned into me, settling into the curve of my arm. Drawing in a deep breath, I steeled myself to say the ugly words. "Whose phone number is that?"

Confusion flickered across her face. "What are you talking about?"

I retrieved the piece of paper from the nightstand where I'd dropped it and placed it in the palm of her hand.

She unfolded it slowly. "Oh, yes. Lorissa said he kept calling like it was some kind of emergency. I took the message to give to you."

I crumpled the note and tossed the paper into the trash bin.

She shifted away from me. "Roman, what did Spitz say to you? It was about me, wasn't it? He doesn't trust me."

"I pay him to be suspicious of everyone, especially now." My guilt continued to swell. What kind of douchebag had I become?

"Including your wife." With a heavy sigh, she moved to the fireplace. The long sheet trailed along the floor behind her. "I get why you're paranoid. Your enemies have left a trail of blood at your feet. You have every right to worry, but not with me. I'm the one person you can trust, Roman. I swear on our unborn child that I'll never betray you."

The darkness I'd been harboring for a lifetime broke loose inside me. "Oh, God." I buried my head in my hands. Unshed tears burned my throat and eyes. Rourke's gentle touch smoothed over my hair.

"It's alright," she murmured as she pressed a kiss to my temple.

Taking her hands in mine, I kissed her knuckles. "Spitz made a very convincing argument." I sought out her gaze, expecting to see anger in her blue eyes, but found them brimming with compassion.

She let out a deep sigh, rose from the bed, and grabbed her phone. "I texted Everly while you were in the bathroom. I wanted to hear the truth from her lips. She might know something that can help us."

"After I told you to stay away from her?" I lifted an eyebrow, amused by her disobedience. "You didn't even wait five minutes."

"I waited thirty. You were with Spitz forever." She opened her text messages, scrolled through the names to Everly's, and handed the phone to me. "Here. You can read them yourself. *Any* of them. Full disclosure."

I curled my fingers around the phone and closed my eyes. In my heart, I believed Rourke. She was the only person I could count on. If I wanted our marriage to work, I needed to take a leap of faith. I handed the phone back to her without looking at it. "No. Your word is good enough for me."

"I've known Everly my entire life. She'd never do anything to hurt me. If she lied about Lavender, I'm sure she has a good reason. I won't pass judgment on her until I hear her side of the story."

"You've known Mr. McElroy your entire life, as well, and I can assure you he's a threat to both of our lives." I tightened my arm around her shoulders and pressed a kiss to her forehead. She leaned into me. The scent of her hair tickled my nose. The warmth of her body melted through the sheet and into my side. "In my experience, the people closest to us are often the most lethal. You need to be cautious. Her father is more dangerous than any of us suspected."

"Thinking back, this explains a lot," she said, tucking a strand of hair behind her ear. "When I went to his house for dinner, he was very insistent that I should divorce you. I thought it was a little strange at the time but figured he was just being overprotective."

My heart skipped a beat at the mention of divorce. I took her hand in mine and lifted it to my lips. "You haven't changed your mind, have you?"

"No." She smiled, bringing light into my world once again. "Of course not."

I eased her back onto the bed and stretched alongside her. With my hand on her belly, I rubbed a circle, encompassing our baby. "Thank goodness. This little guy—or girl—needs me."

"Hey." She propped her head on an elbow and turned on her side to face me. "I just thought of something. If he's really behind all this trouble, maybe I could do a little undercover work."

"No." I lowered the sheet to bare her breasts and placed a kiss on the tip of each one. "You're too valuable. I won't take chances with your safety."

"I'm serious." She dug her fingers into my hair, guiding my mouth to her breast.

I melted into the warmth of her body. Soon, her breasts and belly would get bigger, and I couldn't wait. "You're the most precious thing in my life, and I won't take any more risks where you're concerned. Understand?"

"I guess." With warm hands, she lifted my face to hers, and dotted soft kisses on my forehead and cheeks. "Promise you won't be one of those overbearing, overprotective husbands."

"Can't do it." I shifted my weight above her and teased her legs open with my knee. "It's not in my nature. You'll just have to accept me the way I am."

Her contented sigh gusted against my temple. "Where's the compromise in that, Mr. Menshikov?"

"I'll try. That's the best I can do. Deal?"

"It's all I could ever ask." She raised her hips. The blue of her eyes met mine, filled with heat and desire and the answer to all my prayers.

In one gentle push, I slid inside her. We made love again, slowly and gently. Her sweet moans brought the protective warrior out from the depths of my soul. With her at my side, I could conquer the world.

CHAPTER 18
ROURKE

The next day, I met Everly for lunch. We took turns picking locations; this time was her choice. She settled on an upscale, formal Italian restaurant in Chelsea. I preferred more casual pubs and bistros, but today, the dark, cool atmosphere suited my mood. My stomach twisted with nerves as I followed the maître d' to our table.

Everly glanced up from her phone and greeted me with a smile. She looked amazing in a clingy jersey knit dress. Sunlight from the windows next to our table caught the gold strands in her red hair.

"Hey. Sorry I'm late," I said. "Traffic was insane."

"I just got here myself." She stood and gave me a light hug. The scent of Prada perfume lingered in her wake. I stiffened at her touch.

One of our four waiters pulled out my chair. He snapped open the linen napkin and draped it across my lap. The quiet hum of conversation floated around the dining room. Through the arched windows, the waters of the Hudson River gleamed in the afternoon sun.

"The chicken piccata is amazing here," she said, perusing the menu.

My stomach growled then twisted into a tight knot. On the car ride to the restaurant, I'd played this scenario through a dozen times, trying to formulate a way to approach her about Mr. McElroy, and had come up with nothing but feelings of sadness and pain. We'd vowed to end the secrets between us. So how could she sit calmly across from me, knowing he'd betrayed his family, possessing knowledge that might clear Roman's name, and not say anything? The Everly of my past would never have been a party to that kind of betrayal. I bit my cheek to keep an angry burst of words from spewing forth.

"Would you like champagne or wine?" asked the sommelier. "I can recommend a delightful house cabernet or a vintage pinot, if you're interested."

"Yes, please," Everly said. "I'll have a glass of the cabernet to start, and whatever you recommend to go with my entree."

"None for me, thank you." I fiddled with my napkin, unable to meet her gaze. Confronting her was going to be more difficult than I'd thought, especially since we'd been on such shaky ground the past few weeks. If she continued to harbor her secrets, she'd force me to walk away from our friendship. Tears pricked behind my eyelids. Without her, I'd have no one, no one but Roman. I'd already lost too many important people in my life. I couldn't bear another one.

"Aren't you going to miss wine?" she asked.

I shook my head and stared at the menu.

She ran a hand through the long, glossy locks of her hair, smoothing them over her shoulder. "We won't be able to meet for drinks anymore either. We'll have to find something else to do. Maybe we could go for a walk or shop for baby things." She pressed her delicate, pale hands together. "Oh my gosh. Wait until Christian finds out. He'll be in baby heaven. You have to let him help you with the nursery."

"You're freaking me out." I had so many tasks to complete before the baby arrived. The enormity overwhelmed me. I pushed down the flood of panic. "I don't know anything about children, do you?" My voice sounded rusty. I cleared my throat. Having no siblings, nieces, or nephews had robbed me of the experience.

"No, but you can take classes and hire people who do."

"My children won't be raised by nannies." Roman and I hadn't discussed anything but generalities. We needed to nail down specifics, like his views on discipline, religion, and education.

"Okay." She blinked at my abrupt tone and drew her bottom lip between her teeth. The waitress arrived to take our orders for the meal. Everly waited for the girl to leave before launching a direct attack. "Alright. What's up? Why are you acting so weird?"

Between the two of us, Everly had always been more forthcoming than me. I preferred to linger in the shadows, keeping my heart guarded and safe, while Everly flitted through the light, her wishes and dreams available for anyone to see. I knew when she'd gotten her first period, the first time she'd kissed a boy, to whom she'd lost her virginity. When had all that changed and why had I missed it?

I glanced up to find her watching me with narrowed eyes. "I'm just a little frazzled. I've got a lot going on right now, you know?" To cover my awkwardness, I took a drink of water from the crystal goblet.

"I'll give you that." The creamy skin on her forehead wrinkled. "How is Roman? Are you guys talking yet?"

"He's fine. And yes, we're talking." The genuine concern in her voice brought a lump to my throat.

"Oh, sweetie, that's good, right? At least you've opened up

communications." She reached across the table to place her hand on top of mine. I withdrew my hand and dropped it in my lap. Her eyebrows drew together.

"We still have a lot of ground to cover before he comes back home." I lifted my chin and tried not to think about the photos of her talking to Lavender. "The police searched our penthouse yesterday." From beneath my lashes, I watched for her reaction.

The color drained from her face. "That's terrible."

"It made me sick. You should have seen the way they tore the place apart. They dumped all the drawers on the floor, rooted through my lingerie, everything we own."

She rolled her lips together and looked away. "What were they looking for?"

"Anything to tie Roman to Lavender's murder. They're desperate to indict him. He says it's just a scare tactic, but I find it hard to believe a judge would issue a warrant without probable cause."

"But he'll get out of it, right?" She'd been about to take a sip of wine but lowered the glass back to the table. "A man like Roman has to have a dozen attorneys to protect him, and he's not guilty, there's that." Her voice trailed away, like she was trying to convince herself. "I'm sure it'll all blow over in a few days."

"This isn't going away." I bit the inside of my cheek, pausing to choose my words carefully. "Someone has already tried to assassinate him. They beat up his face. Now they're trying to pin a murder on him. If anything, the situation is escalating. He says it's an attempt to get him under control."

"Oh." She exhaled, the sound gusting between us. Her hand trembled as she lifted her wine glass. The telltale sign added to my confusion. Was she frightened or nervous?

"If anything happens to him, I don't know what I'll do."

Tears pricked the backs of my eyelids. I blinked them away. "I can't let that happen, Everly."

A waiter approached to bring our salads. Once he'd left, she picked up a new thread of conversation. "Does Roman know about the baby? Did you tell him?"

"Yes. He's thrilled." A flush of heat climbed my throat at the memory of his kisses to my belly and the fierce pride in his eyes.

"I knew he would be," she said, her voice unusually thick. "You're going to have a fairytale family."

"I'm sure the baby will enjoy visiting him in prison." Bitterness oozed from the statement. Why didn't she say something about her father's relationship with Lavender and end my misery?

"Rourke!" Her fork dropped to the plate with a clatter, turning a dozen pairs of eyes in our direction. She lowered her voice and leaned forward. "It'll never happen. Don't talk that way."

"You don't know that." Maybe if I pressed her harder, preyed on her sympathies, she'd come clean. "There aren't any guarantees." She stared at the salad in front of her. "I'm happy to be pregnant, but the idea of bringing up a fatherless child breaks my heart." One of the tears escaped and rolled down my cheek. I swiped it away. Everly's eyes welled also. I was getting to her. "Do you think your father could help? Maybe he knows someone or could offer some advice?"

"I doubt it. You know how he feels about using his status for personal gain." Uncharacteristic anger laced her tone. I'd never heard her speak of him with anything less than the utmost respect. Maybe I'd imagined it? Their father-daughter bond had been unshakable.

"Did you have a falling out?"

Before she could answer, the hors d'oeuvres arrived. I watched her from beneath my lashes. If she suspected my dishonesty, she didn't show it by word or action. I used the silence to shovel three small cucumber sandwiches into my mouth. Even though I'd thrown up twice an hour earlier, I was now famished. Roman had held my hair and washed my face with a cool cloth afterward. The memory of his tenderness filled my chest with love.

"Let's just say dear Dad and I had a clash of opinions and leave it at that." A glower darkened her features.

"Did he give you crap about Nicky?"

"No, although he hates Nicky with a passion." She waved a dismissive hand through the air. "You know Daddy. He thinks I'm still ten. It's frustrating. I don't want to talk about it."

"At least you still have him around." Thoughts of my father's sweet smile and corny jokes carried equal measures of sadness and warmth. "My dad wasn't perfect either. He bankrupted us twice. Still, I'd give anything to have him around to meet Roman and see our children."

"I know. You're right. I should be grateful." But her tone suggested otherwise. Her face fell. She toyed with the napkin in her lap. "He yelled at me, Rourke. He's never raised his voice to me—ever." After a heavy sigh, she shook her head. "I can't talk about it."

"Maybe you'll feel better if you get it off your chest." I reached for a fourth sandwich.

"I see the situation hasn't dulled your appetite." A corner of mouth curled up in a teasing smile.

"Sorry. Do you want some?" I nudged the final sandwich toward her. "They're very tiny. I could eat four more."

"Yes, but I'm afraid you'll gnaw my arm if I get too close." We both laughed, easing some of the tension. Even though I was angry with her, the bonds of our friendship tugged at me. They were interwoven tightly into the fabric of my being. I couldn't imagine life without her, although, I might have to.

She shook her head and pushed the plate back across the table. "Go ahead. I can see you're starving."

"Thanks." I finished the final sandwich and motioned for a waiter. "Could we have some more of these, please?" He bowed and headed in the direction of the kitchen. I used the silence to contemplate my next move. I didn't want to risk offending her. On the other hand, I needed answers. The waiter returned with a second tray of sandwiches. I nodded to Everly. "Go ahead. I promise not to bite you."

"Are you sure?" Her laughter ended abruptly. The pale complexion of her skin transformed from ivory to scarlet. "Oh no. Great. Just great." Grabbing her wine goblet, she drained it to the bottom and motioned for the waiter to refill the glass.

"What?" I followed her gaze across the room.

Heads snapped to view the former Vice President. Murmurs of admiration and approval floated through the air. Mr. McElroy caught sight of us and strode in our direction. Nicky and Prince Heinrich trailed behind him.

It was my turn to flush. "Crap."

"I can't do this. I'm going to the ladies." She shoved her chair back with such force that it almost fell over. A passing busboy caught it before it hit the floor.

I grabbed her hand to prevent her escape. "Everly, don't you dare. You've never been a coward. Show Nicky and your father how strong you are."

Our eyes met. Torture and pain filled her pretty eyes, followed by a flash of defiance. "You're right. Screw them both." She flashed a smile. In a louder voice, she said, "Excuse me. I'm so sorry. I thought I saw a spider." By now, the men had reached the table.

"You've always been terrified of bugs. Hello, dear." Mr. McElroy bent to kiss her cheek. She stiffened visibly. He straightened. "Some things never change."

"No, they don't," she replied. Tension laced her words. A tight line of annoyance crossed her lips.

"Rourke, a pleasure, as always." He placed a hand on my shoulder and squeezed. Once, I'd been thrilled by his attentions, but today, his touch sent a shiver down my back. "Let me introduce you to my colleagues. Prince Heinrich, this is Rourke Menshikov. Rourke, this is the Crown Prince of Androvia. And you know Nicky, of course."

"It's an honor to meet you," Henry said in his posh British accent. I extended a hand, unsure if I should bow or curtsey or remain seated. He clasped my fingers between his palms and studied me with the most intense pair of eyes I'd ever seen. Heat raced into my cheeks at the memory of that same gaze watching me have sex with Roman at the Devil's Playground NYC. "Menshikov? Are you related to Roman?" He flicked a curious glance in Nicky's direction. I waited for him to connect the dots, but his expression remained polite and unrevealing.

"They're married," Nicky replied, not bothering to hide his disapproval.

"I wasn't aware Roman had a wife," Henry said.

Nicky snorted. "Where have you been? Under a rock?" I shot him a look of censure, intending to incinerate him with my gaze. He cleared his throat and glanced away, guilt shadowing his eyes.

The prince withdrew his grasp from mine and turned his attention to Everly. "And who is this lovely young lady?"

"This is my daughter, Everly." Mr. McElroy's jaw ticked, his gaze bouncing between Everly and the prince.

"Ah, yes, the delightful Ms. McElroy. I've heard so much about you." Henry took her hand in his and bent low to kiss her knuckles. "You're even lovelier than your reputation."

I didn't like the way his cunning gaze roved over her face or the way his thumb brushed along the back of her hand.

She'd been at the Devil's Playground NYC on the same night as Heinrich. He'd seen her there, but she hadn't noticed. She'd been too busy getting debauched by Nicky at the time.

"Good afternoon, Everly," Nicky said, looking at me and not her.

She winced at the snub, a movement imperceptible to anyone but me.

I corralled my irritation but couldn't hide my scowl. After our little talk, he could at least try to be civil to her. A five-star restaurant, however, wasn't the place to singe Nicky's ears. Later, when I had him alone, I'd unload my wrath on him. I shook my head, enough to warn him about my displeasure. He swallowed. Understanding dawned in his eyes.

"What brings you to New York, Prince Heinrich?" Everly turned a flirtatious smile to the prince. Sexual attraction crackled between His Royal Highness and my best friend. "I'm disappointed our paths haven't crossed sooner."

"Business with your father brought me into the city, but I have a house here, as well. Two, actually." He glanced up at the ceiling and frowned. After a second, he shrugged and smiled, bringing to life the deep dimples beside his mouth. He continued to stroke her hand with his thumb. "I can't keep track anymore."

"That's a terrible problem to have." Her smile widened into genuine amusement.

"Perhaps you'd like to visit sometime. I'm thinking of throwing a dinner party before I head back to Androvia for the summer."

"I'd like that." They beamed at each other, an overwhelming portrait of good genetics and beauty.

Mr. McElroy cleared his throat, stepping between the prince and Everly, forcing him to release his hold on her. "I didn't mean to intrude on your lunch, my dears. I just wanted to stop by and say hello."

"It's good to see you again," I said, almost choking on the untruth. My brain scrambled, desperate to gain a foothold on the mountain of his treachery. "Before you go, do you think you could set aside some to speak with me later? I could use your advice." Maybe I could learn something of use to Roman if we had a moment alone.

CHAPTER 19
ROURKE

r. McElroy's eyes, so like Everly's, flickered with interest. "My door is always open for you, Rourke. Call my assistant. He'll put you on my schedule." He shuttered the predatory gleam and nodded to his companions. "Well, we won't take up any more of your time. It was good to see you, girls. Gentleman, shall we?" Taking control of his guests, he gestured toward the hostess waiting patiently to seat them.

"It's been an honor to meet you both." Prince Heinrich bowed gracefully, his gaze filled with open admiration for Everly. "I look forward to getting better acquainted, Ms. McElroy."

"Go ahead. I'll catch up to you," Nicky said to his companions. "I need to speak with the ladies for just a minute."

"I was just going to the powder room." Everly tried to leave her seat, but Nicky dropped a hand to the back of her chair, halting her escape. She groaned and shook her head, anger punctuating her words. "I have nothing to say to you, asshole."

"I deserve that." His fingers flicked over the knot of his tie. "Please wait. One minute. That's all I ask." Reluctantly, she slid back onto the plush, red velvet seat.

"If you're going to spew out more bullshit, I'm not interested either," I grumbled through gritted teeth.

"Not everything is about you, Mrs. Menshikov." Disdain dripped from his voice. He faced Everly, took her hand, and squeezed it between his palms. "I want to apologize for my behavior toward you. It was inexcusable. I treated you badly, and I'm ashamed. If I led you on, I'm sorry. I hope you won't see my actions as a reflection on your value as a person. You're kind, beautiful, and deserve much more than I could ever give. We both know I'm not the sort of man you want in your life. I hope we can start over and be friends."

Everly and I stared at him, our mouths agape. I'd never seen him contrite before. Sincerity reinforced his words. I blinked, certain this had to be another one of his schemes.

"I—I—don't know what to say." Disbelief clouded her eyes. She glanced at me.

I lifted my eyebrows and shook my head, totally bewildered.

He flashed his mega-watt smile. "We're going to run into each other from time to time. I don't want you to be uncomfortable because I'm a dick. Say you forgive me, and let's move on."

"I can live with that," she said.

This example of her loving nature knotted my insides with indecision. I swallowed and glanced down at my lap. Had I become too jaded?

"Thank you." Nicky's attention returned to me, expression stiffening. I squared my shoulders and prepared for verbal battle. "I hear you're back with Roman. You just don't listen, do you?"

"Unfortunately for you, your credibility is shit with me." I kept my voice pleasant but edged my words with steel. "Nothing you say will ever convince me to leave him. New information has swayed my opinion of Roman's situation."

"What do you know?" Nicky placed both hands on the table and bent low enough to keep his words for my ears only. "You'll give me answers."

I stood abruptly, mimicking his pose, meeting his gray eyes with equal intensity. "I'll give you nothing, Mr. Tarnovsky. In case you've forgotten our last conversation, I meant every word of what I said." He blinked and straightened but didn't look away. I leaned forward. "Don't push me."

"Is everything okay, Mrs. Menshikov?" The maître d' hovered at my elbow. Curious stares burned into my backside. I didn't give a fuck what the other patrons thought. Nicky had toyed with my head for the last time.

"It's alright, Franky. Family squabbles. Mrs. Menshikov and I love to spar." Nicky lifted both hands in the air, his stare still locked with mine. "I was just leaving." He retreated to Mr. McElroy's table on the opposite side of the room, his strides confident, posture straight and proud.

I turned to the maître d'. "Next time, I'd like a more private table. Do you think you could help me with that, Franky? I'd really appreciate it." The judgmental stares of strangers were beginning to wear on my nerves.

"I'm so sorry, Mrs. Menshikov." He brushed imaginary bread crumbs from the pristine table linen and snapped his fingers for a waiter to assist me with my chair. "I apologize for the oversight. I had no idea you were joining Ms. McElroy this afternoon, or I would've seen to it. I can assure you it won't happen again. Would you like to move now?"

"We're fine for today." His statement finally registered in my overtaxed brain. "My husband has private tables here?"

"Yes, madam. He owns the restaurant."

Everly tittered from behind her napkin. "Of course he

does," she said. I shot her a warning glare. She bit her lower lip but couldn't hide her grin. "Roman Menshikov is everywhere."

Roman might enjoy all the fussing, but I'd never get used to it. Sometimes I longed for the days of anonymity when I could grab a hamburger in a fast food chain without four security guards and a crowd of onlookers. However, if I had the power at my fingertips, I might as well make use of it. "We don't need special treatment, Franky. Just privacy."

"No worries, madam. It's a pleasure serving you." Taking a cue from my raised eyebrows, he backed away. I exhaled in relief as he turned to greet a newly arrived pair of patrons.

"So many crazy things just happened there that I don't even know how to begin processing them," Everly said.

"You and me both."

"Do you think Nicky really meant what he said?"

"Who knows." He stared at us from across the room. *Traitor*, I mouthed to him. One corner of his mouth curled up. "He's like a bad little schoolboy who never learns his lesson."

"I don't know. He seems sincere." Her fork hovered in midair between bites of her chicken piccata. "But then again, I obviously can't read him very well."

"He's a mystery, that's for sure." I stared at the plate of pasta in front of me. From my perspective vision, I caught sight of Prince Heinrich staring unabashedly at Everly. "The prince—he's gorgeous, isn't he? I don't think I've ever seen dimples that deep on a man."

"Who? Nicky?" A blush pinked her cheeks. Judging by the electric blue of her eyes and the way they followed Nicky across the room, she still had feelings for him.

"No. Heinrich. He certainly seems taken with you."

"He's okay, I guess, if you like the whole Scandinavianslash-Viking thing." She sighed. "Daddy hates him. The way he talks, you'd think the prince was the anti-Christ."

I bit the inside of my cheek, thinking of the polite way Heinrich had approached me at the Devil's Playground NYC. He'd seemed genuine then, but now I had to wonder. My view of the world and everyone in it had jaded considerably. "I can only imagine what he has to say about Roman."

She motioned to the waiter for more wine. The gold liquid splashed into the goblet. She lifted the glass and stared into its depths. "Daddy's never expressed an opinion of Roman in front of me. Although, he had a dozen questions about him after you came for dinner."

"Like what?" I sat up straighter and leaned forward.

"I don't know—random things, like had I seen the inside of his study, does he entertain a lot of Russian friends, does he take a lot of trips, who runs his security now that Ivan's gone."

"What did you say?"

"I told him I have no idea." She folded her napkin and laid it next to her half-eaten plate.

"Don't you think those questions are kind of weird?"

"Not really. He's so competitive, especially with anyone as young and successful as Roman. He probably wants to update his security or something." She waved a manicured hand through the air. "I try to ignore him."

The prince noticed my stare and smiled. I nodded and glanced away, embarrassed to have been caught watching him. "The prince saw you in the dungeon with Nicky at the Playground."

"No." The color in her cheeks escalated from pink to scarlet. "Are you sure?"

"Absolutely."

"Oh my gosh." With a groan, she buried her face in her hands. "Shoot me now."

"Maybe he didn't recognize you." I tried to bolster my words with reassurance.

She laughed, tossing her head back and revealing her straight white teeth. "With this hair?" She pointed to the shimmering locks. "Fat chance."

"Well, at least he signed an NDA."

"You know, the thing about those nondisclosure agreements is that everyone knows everyone else." She bit her lower lip. "They probably sit around talking about us the way we talk about them."

"Please don't say that." My blood pressure rose a few points at the notion. "Most of the members are too high-profile to discuss the Playground with outsiders. And at least we don't have to worry about leaks to the media."

"True."

We glanced in unison at the three men. From the scowls on their faces, the topic of conversation was less than pleasant. Mr. McElroy thumped a hand on the table, drawing Heinrich's attention away from Everly. Nicky's usual smirk had faded to a more serious light.

"Do you have any idea what they're talking about?" I asked.

"From the little bits and pieces I've overhead, Daddy and the prince are bidding against each other for the same company or piece of property or something." Her explanation didn't account for Nicky's presence.

My phone vibrated with an incoming text from Roman. I glanced at the screen and lifted a finger. "Hold that thought."

Roman: I want you in my office on your knees in thirty minutes.

I felt the blood rush into my cheeks as I tapped out a quick reply.

Me: It's a date.

"That's Roman. I need to go." I signaled for the check. Although our lunch had been eventful, she hadn't volunteered any useful information. Disappointment weighed down my mood. She'd had an entire hour to come clean about her dad but hadn't offered up any insights into his affair with Lavender. I swallowed the hurt, pushed my chair back from the table, and gathered my purse. "Lunch is on me today."

She trotted after me. "Rourke, wait." By the time I reached the door, she'd caught up to me. "What's wrong? Have I done something?"

Her question offered the perfect opportunity to confront her, but I couldn't bring myself to do it. If she was truly my friend, if she truly cared, she would've confessed without prompting. I shook my head and gave her a sad smile. "You tell me. Is there something you're keeping from me, Everly?"

"No. Of course not." Her demeanor chilled. The aura of warmth that usually surrounded us dissipated into the guarded distance of unfamiliar friends. She back away. "Have a great day. I'll see you later."

CHAPTER 20
ROURKE

On the ride to Roman's office, my emotions swayed from hurt to anger and landed on sorrow. To lessen the pain of Everly's betrayal, I focused my thoughts on the connection between McElroy, Nicky, and Prince Heinrich. Finding three of Roman's most dangerous allies at lunch made the hairs lift on the back of my neck, and I was eager to hear his take on the situation.

Behind his enormous desk, he looked devilish in a black suit, black shirt, and silver tie. He was on the phone, speaking into the Bluetooth earpiece, in rapid-fire Russian. His hair brushed the top of his collar, longer than usual, and he hadn't shaved. The space between my legs pulsed at the sight of him.

"Come in." He motioned for me to approach.

I ignored the seats across from his desk and went straight to his side, swiveled his chair to face me, and settled on his lap. With an index finger, he tapped his cheek. I pressed a kiss to the spot.

The corners of his mouth turned up, but he didn't miss a beat of his conversation.

"I missed you," I whispered and stroked his hair.

He shook his head, placing a finger to his lips, warning me to stay silent. The stress and strain of the past few months had stolen a few pounds of weight from him, giving his features a fierce sharpness. The stubble of his beard scratched along my palms. Touching him awakened my desire. When I dotted kisses along his square jaw, he exhaled through his nose, as if summoning his self-control.

Troublemaker, he mouthed.

I winked then slipped from his lap to the floor, kneeling between his widespread knees. The blue of his eyes darkened to black as I slid my hands up his thighs, unfastened his belt, and lowered the zipper of his trousers. When I freed his cock from the opening of his silk boxers, its hard length pulsed against my hand. He ran his tongue across his bottom lip. I liked the way he watched me, knowing he was speaking with someone on the other side of the world. The liquid consonants and harsh Russian speech made my blood sing.

One of his large hands reached down to caress my face. I circled my tongue around the crown of his dick. He tasted of salt and musk. His face contorted when I took him fully in my mouth. The tip of his cock nudged the back of my throat. I swallowed to delay the gag instinct, digging my fingers into the soft fabric of his trousers. The cadence of his speech stuttered. A sense of power surged through me. I liked knowing he couldn't concentrate because of me. Finally, he brought the teleconference to an abrupt end by disconnecting the call and groaned.

"You have no idea what you do to me," he murmured. The softness of his expression filled me with warmth. "Your mouth feels so good. Don't stop." He closed his eyes and leaned his head against the back of the chair. "I won't take long."

Knowing a thousand employees lurked outside his closed

office doors made me feel deliciously dirty and naughty. I sucked harder just to hear him groan.

The rough fibers of the rug dug into my knees, but the discomfort didn't bother me. I wanted to give him pleasure, the way he did for me. He worked too hard for someone so young. His troubles had added lines around his eyes and mouth. Once our lives got back to normal, I was going to make sure he took better care of himself. Visions of long vacations on exotic beaches filled my head. Just me, Roman, and our kids.

The intercom buzzed, and Lorissa's voice floated into the quiet. "Mr. Menshikov, Mr. Spitz is here to see you."

"Damn it." Roman pressed the speaker button. Through gritted teeth, he replied, "Tell him to come back later."

"He insists, sir. I told him you were in a meeting with Mrs. Menshikov, but he said to interrupt."

After a long sigh, he placed a gentle grip on each of my arms and guided me off the floor.

"Two more minutes."

"Sorry, princess. Duty calls."

"That's got to be uncomfortable." I nodded toward his angry erection, bobbing above the black linen of his trousers.

He tucked himself into his underwear. "I imagine whatever he has to tell us will make it go away."

"I need a minute." I stepped into the adjoining bathroom to tidy my hair and reapply lipstick. By the time I returned, the softness had been robbed from Roman's demeanor. His shoulders were straight and tense. A muscle pulsed in his cheek. I headed toward one of the chairs near his desk, but he lifted a hand to stop me.

"No. Over here. I want you where I can touch you." He patted the tops of his thighs, below the obvious tent in his pants.

"You're incorrigible, Mr. Menshikov."

"You have no idea." His mogul façade broke long enough for him to place a kiss on the tip of my nose. "Tell Mr. Spitz to come in," Roman snapped into the intercom.

The wide double doors opened. Spitz strode into the room, wearing a charcoal suit and black tie. His salt-and-pepper hair had been trimmed and the scruff removed from his cheeks.

Roman glowered at him. "You've cockblocked me twice in twenty-four hours, Spitz. This had better be good."

"Sorry, boss." He nodded to me in greeting.

I tried to corral feelings of irritation. It wasn't hard to guess why he didn't like me. He thought I was a traitor and money whore. Knowing he had Roman's best interests at heart lessened some of my animosity. I'd have to win his trust, something earned by time and experience. Few men had the balls to defy Roman. I admired Spitz for standing his ground and taking my husband's safety to heart.

Roman encircled an arm around my waist and pulled me closer. "Go on, Spitz. I've got a million things on my plate today."

"You need to turn on the TV." He nodded toward the wall of flat-screen televisions hidden behind the paneling.

Roman handed the remote control to me. With a press of the buttons, the sliding doors of the console opened. I punched in the news channel and focused on the screen, my mouth open.

A female news anchor spoke into the camera. "—the name of Roman Menshikov, transportation billionaire and exiled price of Kitzeh, has been linked to the death of Lavender Cunningham by unnamed sources. The party planner to the rich and famous was found dead in her Manhattan apartment early last week."

Paparazzi photographs of Roman and Lavender flashed across the television. A much-younger Roman stood on the deck of a yacht, shirtless and wearing low-slung board shorts. The wind ruffled his dark hair. His arm looped around the waist of a bikini-clad Lavender.

I exhaled and breathed through the burn of jealousy at the way they smiled at each other. Roman's jaw tensed, the muscles below his cheekbone flickering. He glanced at me from the corners of his eyes.

The reporter continued. "Speculation surrounds the circumstances of her death. Although authorities refused to comment on the case, a source close to the victim says she had recently argued with Menshikov over his marriage to personal assistant, Rourke Donahue." An unflattering picture of me spun into the center of the screen. I'd been caught in the rain and splashed by a passing car as I stood on the sidewalk outside our apartment building. My hair hung in limp tangles on my shoulders, and the wet material of my blouse clung to the lumps and bumps of my figure.

Roman took the remote from my hand and clicked off the TV. "Don't be upset. Those pictures were taken ten years ago. They had to dig deep to find them."

"It's not that." A knot of growing panic twisted in my stomach. "You said you argued about the Playground. Did you argue about me too?" When Roman didn't answer right away, I tried to wriggle away from him. "Answer me."

"Calm down. No. I'd never discuss you or our marriage with an outsider. I didn't owe her any explanations."

"Who do you think is their source?" Spitz asked.

Roman pursed his lips and frowned. "I have no idea. I'm sure it was a plant by whomever is out for my blood right now." He kept a firm grip on my waist. His words calmed me, but I couldn't shake the feeling of unease. "If you're worried about what people think, don't be. I have an entire publicity department to make these kinds of things go away. They'll take care of it." He buzzed Lorissa on the intercom. "Get Hilda in Public Relations for me, would you?"

"Yes, Mr. Menshikov," Lorissa replied.

"I just came from lunch with Everly," I said. "Mr. McElroy was there. He had a meeting with Nicky and Prince Heinrich." Something in Roman's calm facade made me suspect he already knew about the meeting. "Do you think one of them is involved in this?"

Spitz groaned and raked both hands through his hair. "You had lunch after we explicitly told you to stay away from her?"

"Yes, I did." I lifted my chin, meeting his glare. "I didn't go behind Roman's back. He knew."

"This whole deal is a fucking nightmare," Spitz growled. "Do you have any idea what's at stake here? You're jeopardizing your husband's safety."

"Don't talk to me like I'm the enemy. No one cares more about his wellbeing than me," The volume of my voice climbed as I lost control of my temper.

Roman lifted a hand. Beneath his stern expression, I sensed a hint of amusement at my outburst. "Spitz, I don't appreciate your tone. Rourke is able to make her own decisions. If she feels Everly can be trusted, then you need to respect her choices."

"I apologize for being blunt, but I'm trying to do a job here, and the two of you are making it extremely difficult." Frustration roughened his deep voice.

"Deal with it," Roman said, turning his attention back to me. His tone gentled. "Did you learn anything interesting, Rourke?"

I gave them a brief recap of our conversations. "I don't know what they were talking about at their table, but none of them seemed very happy."

"You did good, baby," Roman said, tenderly brushing my

hair over my shoulder. "Spitz is right to be worried. Until this dies down, I think you should be very careful around the McElroys. No more dinners at their house. You can't trust Everly or her father."

"Agreed." I threaded my fingers through his, enjoying their strength and masculinity. His touch lessened some of the heartache over Everly's defection. "I wanted to give her a chance to come to me first, and she didn't."

Spitz scratched his fingers over his jaw. "If McElroy is meeting with Heinrich, it means there are negotiations on the table. Maybe you need to meet with Heinrich and see what he's planning. You can't afford for those two to join forces. He's the reason you're in this mess."

"I'm more concerned about Nicky's presence at that table than anyone else." Roman drummed his fingers on my thigh. "I asked him to monitor McElroy, not hang out with him."

The intercom beeped. "Mr. Menshikov, Hilda from PR on line seven."

He pressed the speaker button. "Hilda, Channel 197 just ran an unflattering piece on me and my wife. Get hold of them and ask them to make a retraction. Be sure to remind them that I own a large percentage of their stock."

"Yes, sir. Right away."

He smiled. "Sometimes it's good to be me."

Spitz cleared his throat. "I hate to rush you, but time is of the essence here, and I've got something else to cover with you."

Roman twirled a finger through the air. "Get on with it then."

Spitz extended his palm. "Mrs. Menshikov, can I have your phone?"

In my hurry to greet Roman, I'd dropped my purse beneath his desk. I dug inside and handed the iPhone to

Spitz. He dropped it to the floor and smashed it with his heel.

I gasped in horror. "What are you doing?"

"Your movements are being monitored through your phone. We found the tracking software during a routine check a few minutes ago." He squatted and swept the bits of plastic and metal into his hand. "Which is one hell of a mystery, because I gave you this phone myself, and it was clean. Have you opened any strange emails or clicked on weird links?"

"Of course not. I'm very careful." I frowned, remembering Ivan's explicit training on the matter.

"Has your phone been out of your sight for any period of time?"

I bit my lower lip, thinking back over the past few weeks, and shook my head. "No. Never. Except—" The memory made my heart plummet. "I dropped my phone in the car a few days ago. Lance found it and returned it to me." The three of us exchanged glances.

"Have you had any issues with him?" Roman asked. "Anything at all?"

"No. Nothing. He's very loyal."

"I'll speak with him," Spitz said, his voice grave and quiet.

"He should be in the hall." I didn't want to believe Lance could betray us. The walls of the room seemed to be closing in, suffocating me.

"Mr. Menshikov?" Lorissa buzzed into the room, her voice floating from the speakerphone. "Sir, Agent Frankel is here to see you."

CHAPTER 21
ROURKE

My world collapsed at the sight of Roman in handcuffs. He stood tall and proud beside Agent Frankel's sedan, expression stoic. The man guided him into the backseat. I hovered on the sidewalk, arms wrapped around my waist, nearly oblivious to the stares of passersby and their flashing cell phone cameras, and fought the urge to cry.

I love you, Roman mouthed through the window. Seconds later, the car merged into traffic. I remained on the sidewalk, staring after it, until Spitz placed a hand on my elbow. Hopelessness swelled in my chest, threatening to crack my ribs.

"Mrs. Menshikov, I need you to come back inside the building, please." He guided me through the revolving doors and into the lobby, away from the cameras.

"Can't you do something?" Numbness settled over me, heavy and oppressive.

"I'm afraid not." He pressed the elevator call button. Defeat flattened the sharpness of his features.

The ascent to Roman's office floor took an eternity. Each passing second felt like a knife blade to my guts. I couldn't stand by and watch Roman being unjustly accused of murder. There had to be something I could do, favors to be called in, or friends who could assist. "What happens now?"

"He'll be booked into the jail and held until his pre-trial hearing. The judge will set bail, and we can—hopefully—get him out." When he looked at me, his gaze held the same disapproval he'd shown earlier. "He's going to need an attorney. The best his money can buy."

We faced the elevator doors. Our reflections in the polished steel stared back at us. "You don't like me."

"No, I don't." He clasped his hands in front of him, legs braced apart. "But I don't have to like you to work for your husband."

"You can think whatever you want about me, but I'm telling you, I'll do anything to help him. I need you to set aside your misgivings for now. We've got to work together on this, for his sake."

"Agreed."

When the elevator doors opened, I straightened my shoulders and prepared to do battle. Employees huddled around the reception desk and turned to gape at us. I met their scandalized stares with confidence, unblinking, until they averted their gazes.

"Back to business everyone. We have work to do."

They scurried back to their cubicles.

"Spitz, I need a new phone ASAP." I strode down the corridor, purpose in my step. He caught up to my side. "Is there anyone you can call to see what's going on?"

"I've got a few contacts."

The heels of my shoes clicked on the pristine tile floor. "Who's the best criminal attorney in the city?"

"Kellie Laghari," he said without hesitation.

I'd heard the name before. She'd recently defended a movie star accused of killing his wife.

I paused at Lorissa's desk. Concern deepened the fine lines around her eyes and mouth. "Is there anything I can do to help, Mrs. Menshikov?" she asked.

"Yes. Get Kellie Laghari on the phone. Tell her it's urgent."

Inside Roman's office, I laid my forehead on the desk, closed my eyes, and cursed. How had things gotten so far from the grasp of our control?

Within a minute, Lorissa called into the room. "Mrs. Menshikov? I wasn't able to get Kellie Laghari on the phone. Her assistant says she's in court today and booked solid for the next thirty days. I left a message. And Everly McElroy is on line two for you."

I drew in a deep breath and tried to push aside the rising tide of panic. "Keep calling Ms. Laghari and get her firm's address. I'll go to her if she won't come to me." Placing a hand over my racing heart, I counted to ten, hoping to regain a semblance of composure before taking Everly's call. "Hey, what's up?"

"I tried to text you. Your phone isn't working. I took a chance that you'd be in the office. I just heard about Roman. It's bad, isn't it?" Her voice, normally quiet and modulated, sounded thin and strained.

"Yes." I rubbed my forehead with two fingers, hoping to ease the dull ache between my temples.

She sighed. "I need to talk to you—in person. It's important."

"I've got a lot going on."

"I'm in front of your building. I'll make it quick." She paused. "Please, Rourke."

Five minutes later, she stood in front of Roman's desk, shifting from one foot to the other. The blue hue of her dress intensified the color of her eyes. Her hands trembled as she smoothed the crown of her long, red hair.

"So what's the emergency?" I asked, unable to hide the hurt of her betrayal. She was supposed to be my best friend, the person I trusted most after Roman.

After an audible intake of air, she said, "The day Lavender Cunningham died, I found out she was having an affair with my dad."

"I know—Spitz has photos of the three of you," I said. She fell silent. I rested an elbow on the desk and gripped my forehead.

"Is that why you were acting so weird at lunch?"

"I was hoping you'd come forward to tell me." We stared at each other. More than anything, I wanted to believe in her motives, to trust her again.

"How long have you known?" She turned her back and walked to the wire-and-metal sculpture hanging on the far wall.

"Since yesterday."

"It's not what it looks like. I swear." She pivoted on her stiletto heels. Her words gathered speed. "I was visiting a friend who lives in Lavender's building and ran into them on the elevator. It was...upsetting to say the least." The pain in her voice thawed some of the ice around my heart. "He didn't apologize or anything. He said his relationship with my mom was solid, and he expected me to be an adult and keep it to myself. They gave me a ride home. We had a huge argument in the car. It was awful." Tears softened the brightness of her eyes. She stopped beside me and placed her hand on mine. "I'm so sorry."

Her anguish brought a thickness to my throat. I stared at our hands. "You're not responsible for his behavior. He's a grown man. I just wish—I wish you'd told me sooner."

"I threatened to tell Mom if he didn't break it off, and that's where we left it. Things have been strained between us since then."

The enormity of her confession hit me with full force. Not only did Mr. McElroy have a motive for Lavender's death, Everly did also. In my heart of hearts, I knew she didn't have the capacity to harm someone, but a spark of anger flared at her reluctance to come forward. "I understand why you didn't say anything, but it might have saved Roman a lot of trouble."

"I know it was wrong." She hung her head. "But it gets worse. He didn't come home at all the night Lavender died. I know, because Mom mentioned it the next day. He left a voice mail for me later and said the situation 'had been resolved' and not to worry my mother with it." She drew air quotes around the words with her fingers.

"Do you think he could do something like that?" Even with photograph evidence of his dalliance, Mr. McElroy still seemed like the all-American hero.

"Of course not." She rolled her eyes.

"You have to tell the police." My pulse began to pound between my temples. I reached for the phone.

"No." She placed a hand on the receiver, blocking me. "Rourke, he's my dad." Her blue eyes grew rounder, reminding me of the way she'd looked as a child.

I studied her downcast face, debating my next move. "I wish you'd trusted me enough to tell me."

"I *do* trust you. More than anyone." Tears continued to gather in her eyes. "That's why I'm telling you now. As much as I love you, I don't want to betray him. Can't you understand? I'm in a tough position." Sincerity rang in her words.

"And Roman is my husband." The futures of two important people depended upon the truth. My frustration continued to escalate. "You'd let an innocent man go to prison for a crime your father committed?"

"It's not going to come to that. If Roman is innocent, his lawyers will prove it."

"*If* he's innocent? *If?* Do you hear yourself?" The cap on my temper exploded. I paced across the room, fighting the urge to throw something. "I don't know who you are anymore."

"We don't know that Dad did anything wrong," she said, frowning. "I'm not going to throw him under bus for no reason. What kind of daughter would do that?"

"But he had the means, motive, and opportunity. His relationship with Lavender would be enough to cast reasonable doubt on Roman." Despite the recent ugliness and deceit introduced into my life, I needed to believe there were still good people in the world. She'd always been a true friend. In the end, I knew she'd do the right thing. "Go to the police, Everly. You have to do this for me."

"And say what? My father, the beloved former Vice President and war hero, had an affair with Lavender?" She lifted her palms into the air. "I don't have any evidence. They'll think I'm insane or out for publicity."

My hopes plummeted. Fate attempted to thwart me at every turn. I closed my eyes. When I opened them, coldness seeped into my bones. "If you don't do this for me, we're done, Everly."

"What?" She jerked as if I'd struck her. "You don't mean that."

"I do mean it. Every word. Either you take care of this, or I will, and I guarantee you won't like my methods."

She left the office, wounded and angry. The old Rourke would have gone home to wallow in misery, but Mrs. Menshikov didn't have time for self-pity. As soon as the door closed behind her, I summoned Spitz.

"Lance has been terminated," he said, expression grim.

"What did he say?"

"Not a damn thing. Just took his paycheck and left." He ran a hand through his grizzled crew cut. "I'll have Graves step in for him. He's a good guy. Served under me in the military."

"Okay. Thanks for handling that."

"And here's a phone for you." He pulled a new iPhone from his pocket. "I had your contacts and email transferred over. You should be ready to go."

We might not like each other, but I had to respect his competency. "Great. I'll need the car brought around. I'm going to Kellie Laghari's office and hound her until she sees me. And do you have those pictures of McElroy and Lavender?"

"Yeah."

"Make two copies. Take a set with you. Put them some-where safe."

"And the other one?"

"That set is for Mr. McElroy. An insurance policy."

His eyebrows lifted to his hairline. "My respect for you has escalated to a whole new level."

CHAPTER 22
ROMAN

Around mid-morning following the day of my arrest, the guard pulled me out of my cell and led me to a visitation room. An unfamiliar man peered at me from beneath unruly black eyebrows. He sat on the edge of the metal table, sipping coffee from a Styrofoam cup. The hem of his pants rode up his legs, showing a swath of hairy calf and black socks. He stood when I entered.

"Mr. Menshikov, I'm Mr. Green. It's a pleasure to finally meet you." A thick Bostonian accent couched his words. "Have a seat."

I pulled out the chair across from him and rubbed my wrists, grateful to be free of the handcuffs.

"Help yourself." He nodded toward a second cup of coffee and a box of donuts. "How'd you sleep last night?"

"Like a baby." I winced as the hot coffee scalded my tongue. Because of my fame, I'd been given a solitary cell, separate from the other inmates. The unfamiliar sounds of the jail and the hard metal bunk had kept me awake, but he didn't need to know that. "You?"

"Great, thanks for asking." His tone was light and conversational, but he watched me with predatory intent. "I was up late watching the Celtics. Are you a basketball fan?"

"Not really."

"No? Too bad. Great game."

"I want my phone call and an attorney." I didn't give two shits about this man in his cheap suit with the broken capillaries around his nose and bad haircut. I wanted to go home to Rourke. Immediately.

"We'll get to that." Green sat on the edge of the desk, crossed his arms over his chest, and regarded me down the length of his hawk nose.

"You're not with the FBI," I said, realizing he'd failed to identify his branch of employment.

"No, I'm not." The soles of his shoes left black scuff marks on the concrete floor. "I'm here on behalf of an independent contractor, a former business associate of yours."

"And who might that be?" I feigned disinterest while my blood pressure began to climb.

"You know I can't name names. Kind of like that kinky club of yours." His thick black eyebrows waggled, mocking me.

"Just get to the point. What do you want?"

"I saw your wife this morning." His lazy smile suggested he enjoyed prolonging my torment. The hairs lifted on the back of my neck. "She's an attractive woman."

My fingers curled with the urge to pin him to the wall by the throat. "Lay one finger on her, and you'll die."

"Are you threatening me, Mr. Menshikov? Because I'd be happy to add a few additional charges to the ones already pending."

"Anyone who knows me knows I don't make threats, Mr. Green."

He shrugged. "From where I'm standing, you're fucked. My employer is a very powerful man, more powerful than you. In fact, he fabricated this little mess to teach you a lesson. If you continue to interfere in his business, he'll take you out the same way he took out Ms. Walenska and your friend Ivan."

"I don't know who your employer is, but you can tell him to kiss my ass."

"Are you sure about that? What you're going through right now is nothing compared to the hell he's prepared to rain down on you and your family if you don't cooperate."

His ominous words knifed through me. It was one thing to gamble with my own life, but another to jeopardize the safety of my wife and children. Their wellbeing meant more to me than my mortality. "I want my attorney." Although I'd been in a cell for almost twenty-four hours, I hadn't been given a phone call nor a visit with legal counsel.

He took a sip of his coffee and regarded me over the rim of his cup. "Give me your word that you'll cut ties with Prince Heinrich, and this can all be over."

"I have no idea what you're talking about." I mimicked his casual pose.

Mr. Green laughed. "I've been given the authority to do whatever is necessary to stop you. I can be very creative when I need to."

"You must have me confused with someone else. I'm just a simple businessman." In a show of bewilderment, I lifted my open palms in the air. "When word gets out that I've been denied my basic rights, your ass is going to be in a world of hurt."

"I'm not worried."

"Well, you should be. I bet my Lear jet that your boss's boss has no idea I'm here. And when he finds out? He's going to be pissed."

"My boss's boss is the President of our great nation."

I shrugged. "Like I said."

Someone banged on the door. Both our heads snapped in the direction of the entrance. "Come in," Green said. "What is it? I'm busy."

The man cast a worried frown in my direction. "Sir, we have an issue."

"Unless the goddam Pentagon is on fire, I don't care." Green returned his attention to me, but the man persisted.

"I think you'll care about this."

At that exact moment, Green's phone buzzed. He frowned at the caller ID before placing the phone to his ear. His expression drooped, and his jaw clenched. "Are you sure?" I couldn't make out the identity of the person on the other side of the line, but they were definitely shouting. "Fine. Right away."

"Your wife?" I asked.

He sighed, a heavy, gusting exhale of a man whose patience had been tried to the limits. "Your attorney is here." He slipped out of the room moments before the door opened for a second time.

A woman stepped into the room—*Kellie fucking Laghari.* We'd never met before but I knew her by reputation and by her frequent television appearances. She nodded to me and extended her hand. "Mr. Menshikov, good to see you. I'm Kellie Laghari. Your wife has retained me as your legal counsel."

"Ms. Laghari, it's a pleasure." We shook hands. Her firm grip encased my fingers. Few people intimidated me, but she became a serious contender for the title. Only a few inches shorter than my six-four, she exuded strength and authority in a severe red power suit and blue-black hair shorter than mine. "I'm glad to see you."

"Please call me Kellie." Her mouth remained in a firm line, but her eyes were filled with warmth. "Have you been mistreated in any way?" Her dark gaze slid over my face, looking for signs of battery.

"Not really. Although I haven't eaten since I arrived, and no one offered me a phone call." I scratched a my fingers through my beard.

"We'll make sure they're held accountable for that." She claimed the chair across from me at the table and pulled a file from her briefcase. "I've spoken with the judge and the District Attorney. Apparently, most of the evidence against you is circumstantial. They're building a case strictly around your DNA found at the crime scene."

"That's not possible." My tired mind fought to process the information. "I haven't been to Lavender's apartment in over two years."

"According to the evidence, they also found a dresser drawer in her bedroom containing personal items identified as belonging to you—clothing, cufflinks, a watch, condoms—all with your fingerprints."

"Like I said, impossible." I ran my hands through my hair.

She thumbed through the paperwork, frowning. "I need you to be honest with me, Mr. Menshikov. Everything you say to me is confidential under attorney-client privilege. Do you have any knowledge of Ms. Cunningham's death?"

"No. Absolutely not."

"And yet, you can't provide an alibi for the night of her murder?"

The walls of the room shrank. "I was at a business meeting with Prince Heinrich Von Stratton."

"All night?" She cocked an eyebrow.

"The prince keeps late hours."

"Can he corroborate your story?"

"He could, but he won't," I said. "The nature of our business was—" I paused, searching for the proper term. "Delicate."

CHAPTER 23
ROURKE

Mr. McElroy greeted me at the door of his home with a smile. "Come in. Come in. Judy said to send you her regrets. She had some kind of luncheon thing today, so it's just the two of us."

"Oh, well, I'll miss her. Be sure to give her my love." Being alone with him in the giant townhouse set my nerves on edge. I glanced down the empty hallways and listened for sounds of the household staff. Silence greeted my ears.

He gestured toward the leather sofa in front of the fireplace. "Make yourself comfortable. I'm glad you reached out to me. I've been worried about you. This business with Roman—it's a terrible thing. You must be horrified."

"It was certainly unexpected." My insides quaked. This wasn't the time for a panic attack. The events of this meeting could shape Roman's future. Why hadn't I formulated some kind of strategy prior to barging over here? I brushed my sweaty palms over the fabric of my skirt before clasping them together in my lap.

"There's no need to beat yourself up about it. A man with Roman's appetites will never be satisfied with just one woman, even one as spectacular as you. I'll do everything in my power to get you out of this mess."

The cherubs and naked women of the ceiling mural stared down at me, judgment in their round, angelic eyes.

Mr. McElroy opened the heavy doors of an antique Italian liquor cabinet and withdrew an elaborately decorated silver box. He lifted the lid to reveal a mirrored interior, matching brandy snifters, and an ornate silver bottle. With his back to me, he filled the glass with an inch of golden liquid. "Would you like some?"

"No. I'm fine, thank you." I sucked in a breath and gathered my courage. "I'm not here about a divorce. I'm here because I know about you and Lavender."

He froze for a fraction of a second then placed the snifter into a warmer fashioned from elaborately intertwined gold vines and lit the tea candle underneath. Except for the ticking of the grandfather clock in the corner and the occasional honk of a car horn from the street, silence filled the room. He placed both hands on the top of the bar and stared at the counter for an eternity before turning to face me. "What, exactly is it that you think you know?" he asked, his tone unexpectedly mild.

"That you had a longstanding affair. That you were at her apartment the night she died. And there are witnesses."

He stared into the brandy, slowly swirling the contents around the glass. "Not anymore."

"What does that mean?" My heart pounded furiously against my chest.

"It means those people no longer exist." He sank into the chair across from me.

A cold chill ran down my back. Although he could have been bluffing, something in his tone suggested otherwise. "I have pictures—photographs—taken from a neighboring security camera."

"I don't believe you." Danger sharpened his words. He rested an ankle on the opposite knee, assuming the pose of a man who feared very little.

I called the pictures up on my phone and flashed them beneath his nose. His expression remained bland, his breathing unhurried. After a minute, he waved my hand away. "Don't underestimate the scope of my authority. I've been playing this game since before you were born. Roman's father tried it, and look what happened to him."

The chill turned into icy fingers, threatening to strangle me. I swallowed and sat back against the plush cushions to do the math. Mr. McElroy was in his seventies. Everly had been a late child from Judy, his much-younger second wife. He would have been in his twenties when Roman's parents had died. I pressed a hand to my mouth, feeling the bile crawl up my throat. "I don't think you should be telling me these things."

"Why not? We're old friends, right? And I trust you." When I didn't answer, he took a sip of the brandy, closed his eyes, and nodded. "Mmmm. Very good. It's Hennessey. Two hundred grand for this bottle. I guarantee you've never tasted anything like it. Are you sure you don't want some?"

"No." My frustration began to grow.

His tone gentled. "Do the right thing here, Rourke. Are you going to cling to this husband of yours, a reject from his own government, a man who deals in weapons and war? Or are you going to side with your country and me, a decorated war veteran and former Vice President?"

I curled my fingers into fists. My nails bit into the flesh of my palms. The pain helped center my thoughts. I forced aside the dismay to be processed at a later date. Right now, Roman was my only focus. "You're pointing fingers at Roman, but you're the dangerous one."

"Not dangerous, Rourke. Committed. Because I'm the

kind of man who gets the job done. You don't think I got to this position without stepping on a few toes, do you?" He shook his head and paused for another sip of brandy. The soft, silky texture of his voice frightened me more than a knife to my throat. "You're playing with fire."

"I'm not playing, sir," I replied. "I set those photographs to go out in a social media blast in an hour." I glanced at the delicate silver watch Roman had given me on my birthday. "Make that fifty minutes."

"Photographs don't mean shit without corroborating evidence." He tapped the thick gold band of his wedding ring against the glass in his hand. The sound, meshed with the ticking grandfather clock, set my frayed nerves on edge. After a few minutes of contemplation, he placed the snifter in the center of the coffee table, rested his elbows on the tops of his thighs, and clasped his hands between his knees. "You know, I like Roman. He's smart, ambitious, and has a cutthroat approach to business—traits I can respect in a man. I'd hoped Ivan's death would be enough to put him back on track, but he jumped ship and sided with Androvia. Needless to say, I'm very disappointed."

The scope of his treachery sucked the wind from my lungs. I tried to inhale through my nose and remain outwardly calm. "I trusted you. You were like a father to me."

"And I've always considered you to be a second daughter." His weighted sigh floated on the air between us. "Here's the thing. I don't take kindly to blackmail. Not from you. Not from anyone. We both want something, so let's get down to business, shall we? I want Roman to end his liaison with Androvia and Kitzeh. If you can get him to cut ties with those countries, I'll have him cleared of all charges."

"Oh, Daddy. No." Everly's voice floated from the doorway. I had no idea how much she'd heard, but the downturned corners of her mouth suggested enough. Or maybe she already knew? Betrayal sliced through my chest, sharp and deep, for a third time.

"What are you doing here?" Remorse flickered in his eyes as his head snapped up.

"Mom said I could borrow her red dress for a charity auction tomorrow night." The vibrant-colored gown dangled over her arm. Her gaze met mine. Hurt and resignation mingled in the depths of her blue eyes.

"How much of that did you hear?" The rough edges of his voice scraped over my ears.

"Enough to know you're not the man I thought you were."

"Don't be naive. Get in here." He rose to his feet and motioned for Everly to join us. "I tried to protect the both of you from the ugliness of my business, but I can see that was a waste of time. You need to grow up. The world is a brutal place made up of leaders and sheep. Where you fall on the spectrum of power is completely up to you."

"Everything you taught me was a lie," Everly said, her voice high and thin with shock as she sank down beside me. "Kindness, honesty, loyalty—you don't represent any of those things."

"Those are noble ideas, but they don't always get the job done. Don't be ungrateful." His voice rose to a thunderous shout. "I've made hard choices—not all of them pretty—to protect my family and country, and I'll continue doing so as long as I've got breath in my body."

"I'm so sorry, Rourke." Everly's face crumpled. "I'm not part of this. I swear."

"I know." I covered my hand with hers, grateful for her declaration.

"Daddy, you need to make this right." The graceful line of her shoulders squared. "If you don't fix this, I'll never speak to you again."

"Don't be melodramatic." The lines of his forehead deepened in a scowl. "We both know you're not serious. Let's see how far you get without an allowance from me."

"I don't give a fuck about your blood money." The quiet fury in her voice caused my head to snap up. Mr. McElroy had always been her hero. I'd never heard her disrespect him.

"Don't take that tone with me," he roared. "Your loyalty lies with me and not her."

"You lost my respect when you cheated on Mother with Lavender, but you lost my loyalty when you threatened Rourke." She squeezed my hand. My heart ached for her. I knew how hard those words were for her. At the same time, I admired her spunk. "Come on, Rourke. We need to go."

I wanted to go with her, but I had my own battles to wage. Roman's fate depended on whatever happened in this room.

"Everly can leave," he said, jerking his chin toward the door. "I'll have Lance drive you home. But Rourke, you and I have business to finish."

"If I walk out that door without Rourke, you've lost me forever," she said.

I sat on the sofa, biting the inside of my cheek, and struggled to contain my surprise.

Mr. McElroy paced the length of the room twice, his expression calm but his agitation belied in the fists curled at his sides.

Lance stepped into the study, a smirk on his clean-shaven face. His eyes met mine at once. "Good afternoon, Mrs. Menshikov."

"I'm disappointed in you," I said quietly. "I liked you."

"And I liked you, too. But Mr. McElroy made me an offer I couldn't resist. I don't intend to be a rich woman's bodyguard for the rest of my life."

"I'm sure." I smiled pleasantly, my sweet tone dripping

with acid. The longer I played their game, the easier it became to follow their rules.

"Lance has been invaluable to me. He kept tabs on you and was able to obtain Roman's DNA from your penthouse," McElroy said and shifted to face me. "Take a lesson, Rourke. It's always good to have an insider on your payroll."

"I'll remember that," I replied. My stomach churned.

"Lance, drive Everly home, would you?"

"No." Everly's tone reeked of obstinance. "I meant what I said. I want nothing more from you."

He shrugged. "Suit yourself."

"Call me when you leave, Rourke, and let me know you're okay," Everly said. Lines of worry bracketed her mouth. "And don't worry. I'll make this right."

"I know you will," I replied.

Mr. McElroy waited until she left the room, Lance trailing behind her, before he spoke. "She's always been a handful, but she'll come around."

"I think you're underestimating her. You always have."

He shrugged. "She'll make a fuss for a short time, but eventually, she'll do as she's told." He steepled his fingers in front of him, his cool gaze locking onto mine. "You know, now that I've had some time to think, I believe I'm done with negotiations. Things will be much simpler for me without you and your husband around." He shook his head. The sinister smirk on his lips made my heart lurch in fear. "You may walk out of here today, but never stop looking over your shoulder. It might be a car wreck. A plane accident. Or, my personal favorite, an active shooter at a restaurant. The options are endless."

I swallowed past the lump in my throat. For the first time, it occurred to me that I might not leave the townhouse alive. Why hadn't I listened to Spitz?

I glanced at the window. Graves was outside with the car

but too far away to hear me if I screamed. On instinct, I pressed a hand to my belly and my unborn child. In an instant, my dreams became crystal clear. I wanted to use the power Roman had offered to make a difference in the world. I wanted to be a wife to him and a mother to his children. The revelation bolstered my courage. I tapped the face of my watch. "Do I need to remind you that the photographs will go viral in thirty minutes?" The inside of my mouth felt dry as cotton. I licked my cracked lips, trying to remain calm.

"Idle threats." His flat gaze met mine, completely devoid of warmth or emotion. "You're too nice, Rourke. You'd never hurt Judy or Everly that way."

"Try me," I replied.

CHAPTER 24
ROMAN

After a healthy contribution to the non-profit organization of the judge's nephew, my bail was set at a million dollars and I was free to go until the preliminary trail. Spitz and Kellie met me at the front of the jail. A throng of reporters, journalists, and TV cameras jostled for positions at the street, eager to sensationalize my story.

"We're going to step outside, and I'm going to make a statement for you." She glanced over me with a critical eye. "The media is on the fence—half of them are screaming for your blood and the other half, the female half, is rooting for you." She straightened my tie and collar with business-like intensity. "Don't speak to anyone. I'll do all the talking. Try to look engaged and confident."

Spitz opened the door. My security team converged on us, shielding me from the wall of onlookers. I winced at the bright sunlight. With cool poise, Kellie stepped up to the microphone. All of the major television stations were present. They shouted questions until she tapped the microphone, requesting silence. I stood behind her, making a point to meet the eyes of each person, hands clasped in front of me, grateful for the fresh air. I searched the crowd for Rourke's blond head. Where was she? In the car?

"Mr. Menshikov will not be making a statement this morning." At the ensuing groans, she lifted a hand. "As his attorney, I'm confident our legal system will acquit him of all charges, and justice will be served. Thank you. There will be no questions."

My men formed a wall around us, herding us to the waiting Maybach. When we slipped into the cool interior of the car, I exhaled a long and heavy sigh. Relief blanketed me, releasing a tension I'd been unaware of before now. Rourke was nowhere to be found. My spirits plummeted.

"Where's my wife?" I asked.

"She went to see McElroy," Spitz replied, his mouth thinning into a line of displeasure.

"And you let her go? What the fuck?" Blood roared through my ears as my blood pressure rocketed. I tapped out a quick text to her: *Where are you? Call me ASAP.*

"For the record, she went without my consent. She's as stubborn as you are." He scratched his freshly shaved chin. "Graves is with her, and her driver. She didn't want to alarm McElroy with an entourage of security."

I gripped my forehead. Pain bounced between my temples.

Kellie studied us, her dark eyes teeming with respect. "Your wife is quite the spitfire, Mr. Menshikov. Not every woman has the balls to show up at my office then throw a fit in my reception area until I agreed to meet her."

"She's one of a kind," I said. My wife had taken control of the situation in a fashion worthy of a war queen. Pride expanded my chest. "She's a force to be reckoned with."

Kellie nodded. "I'm impressed." Her voice lowered. "I'm not sure what you're involved in, Mr. Menshikov, but you're playing a dangerous game with dangerous people. You need to be very careful."

"Your candor is appreciated." I nodded. "And duly noted."

The Maybach drew to a halt in a nearby parking garage. Kellie hesitated before opening the door. "I'm leaving town for a few days, but my aides are working on your case as we speak. Give me a call if you need me. You've got my cell." We shook hands, and she exited the car.

The moment the door closed, I shifted into business mode. "Take me to Rourke." If anything happened to her, I'd never forgive myself. She meant more to me than all the money, cars, and homes in my possession. I'd sacrifice everything to have her in my arms and safe.

"I texted her as soon as you were released, but she hasn't answered. Graves says she's still with McElroy." He studied his phone, brows drawn together over his nose.

"Get me over there. Now."

🌫

THE DRIVE TO McELROY'S TOWNHOUSE TOOK FOREVER. When the driver announced my name at the gate, the guard nodded, as if he'd been expecting me. On the front steps of the house, I rang the doorbell.

A woman, dressed in a black uniform, answered the door. "Good afternoon, Mr. Menshikov. Mr. McElroy would like you to join him and your wife in the study."

I followed her down a wide hall. Generations of McElroys stared down at us from portraits in heavy gold frames. She opened a set of double doors and stepped to one side for me to pass. Rourke sat on one of the twin leather sofas in front of the fireplace, her complexion pale. Her eyes met mine. Relief, joy, and fear greeted me in their soft blue depths. I ignored McElroy, who stood as I entered, and went straight to her side. "Are you okay?"

"Yes. I'm fine. Are you?" She steadied my face between her palms for inspection.

"Absolutely, thanks to you." I pulled her into my embrace and squeezed until she squirmed. The scent of her hair and the softness of her body melted my heart in a thousand different ways. "What are you doing here?"

"She came to negotiate on your behalf." McElroy interrupted our reunion. "And she's doing a damn fine job of it, I have to say."

"Of course she is." I stroked a fingertip along the curve of her cheek.

"Unfortunately, we haven't been able to come to an agreement." He studied us from his position on the sofa. "I'm forgetting my manners. Can I offer you a cigar, Roman, or a brandy?"

"We're not staying," I said. "Time for us to leave, Rourke."

McElroy stood, blocking our path. "Not until we settle this. You owe me seven shipments of weapons, Menshikov."

"I don't owe you shit," I replied, keeping my voice as even as possible. I wanted to crush him beneath the heel of my boot like an insignificant insect, and I would, but not until Rourke was safely out of his reach.

"We both know that's not how this works." He continued to stare at me from beneath his lowered brows. "I give you the payment. You deliver the goods."

"Then you'll be waiting a very long time." I wrapped an arm around Rourke's waist. "Come on. Let's go home."

McElroy remained seated, but called out when we reached the door to the study. "Rourke, remember what I said. It could happen anywhere."

"What did that mean?" I asked as we scrambled toward Spitz and the car.

"He threatened me—us." A tremor wracked her body. I pulled her closer. "He basically said he was ordering a hit on our lives."

"I'll never let that happen." The muscles in my jaw tensed.

"He's too powerful. We'll never be safe." The terror in her eyes filled me with rage. "He was involved in your parents' deaths, Roman. He killed Ivan." She shivered again. "He's pure evil."

The last pieces of the puzzle snapped into place. Hot bile burned my throat. Don McElroy had been the mastermind behind the wars and skirmishes plaguing smaller countries in the Middle East and surrounding Kitzeh. He'd made a fortune by stirring up hatred and dissent among radical factions. My guns had facilitated his wars and made me rich in the process.

Rourke's bare knee brushed mine as she crossed her legs and tugged down the hem of her dress. A surge of need traveled up my thigh and settled in my groin. Her nearness kick-started my starving libido. Her fingers found mine on the car seat between us and curled around my hand, her touch tentative and warm. "Hey," she said, softy. It was only one word, but it held unlimited implications. "Are you okay?"

"Yes." I tugged her closer into my side. Her heart beat steadily against my ribcage. It was the best feeling in the world.

"Roman, I'm scared."

I mustered a smile. "Don't be. In case you've forgotten, I'm the war king, and you're my queen. No one fucks with us and gets away with it."

CHAPTER 25

ROURKE

I wrapped my arms around Roman's neck and held him tight. Waves of emotion wracked my body. Love. Warmth. Desire. I rained kisses on his face and neck. "I love you. I love you." I murmured the words over and over.

"I love you, too." He clutched me tighter against him. The buttons of his shirt pressed into my chest. "You crazy, stubborn, beautiful idiot. You could have been killed, you know that?" His lips brushed my hair.

"I had to do something."

"You're amazing." The warm, softness of his lips dipped to my throat. "Kellie Laghari is the best of the best. How in hell did you pull that off?"

"I practically laid down in her office and threw a tantrum," I said, biting back a smile of embarrassment. "And I offered her two invitations to the Masquerade de Marquis."

"Ah, very nice, Mrs. Menshikov." He sucked on the tip of my earlobe. Waves of pleasure skittered along my nerve endings, settling in my nipples and between my thighs. His tongue flicked over the shell of my ear. "All this talk of blackmail and payoffs is making me hard."

I dropped a hand to his crotch and palmed the steely length of his erection. "Do we have time for a quickie?"

He wrapped my fingers around the outline of his cock and pushed into my hand. "We have all the time in the world."

Spitz's voice floated over the intercom from the front seat. "Hey, boss?"

"No," Roman said tersely. His eyes darkened to midnight blue. "Whatever it is, it can wait."

"I just received a text from Mr. Tarnovsky. He said there's a media shit storm going on right now. You need to turn on your television."

Roman sighed. "Fuck." He released me and scrubbed both hands over his face with a male growl that sent a pulse of electricity into my core. "Alright."

I handed the remote control to him, and he flicked on the TV to a local news station.

The camera panned to a reporter stationed in front of McElroy's gated community. "—photographs showing former Vice President Don McElroy in intimate proximity to murder victim Lavender Cunningham. A source close to the Vice President has confirmed that the decorated war veteran was in a long-term relationship with Ms. Cunningham at the time of her death. Mr. McElroy has not responded to our attempts to obtain a statement."

"Who do think is the source?" Roman asked, weaving his fingers through mine.

"Everly." I dug my phone out of my purse, remembering my promise to text her, and typed in a message. She didn't reply. "She heard almost everything Mr. McElroy said."

"If she comes forward with information against her father, her life will be as much at risk as ours." His grave tone sent a shiver down my back. "He might not hurt her, but he'll find a way to shut her up."

"We can't let that happen." I cupped his cheek in my

hand, enjoying the scratch of his five o'clock shadow on my palm.

He pressed a kiss to the center. "Anything you want, my queen. Like I said before, all you have to do is ask." Heat illuminated his eyes. I loved it when he looked at me that way, like he couldn't get enough of me.

I grinned and pressed the driver call button. "Drive us around the park once before we go home."

"What have you got in mind?" Roman asked, his voice growing deeper, edged with just enough roughness to make my panties dampen.

"You'll see." I eased his zipper down before straddling his hips. His cock jumped forward. I nudged the panel of my panties aside and dragged his crown through my wetness.

The breath hissed out of him. "I'm scandalized. You realize it's the middle of the day?" He cocked an eyebrow, a smile twitching his mouth.

"You said I could have anything I want. Well, I want you. Now." To emphasize my point, I eased onto his erection, taking him in halfway before stopping.

"Jesus." The strangled tightness of his exclamation rewarded my efforts. "You're so wet."

The smooth leather of the seats warmed beneath my bare legs. I lowered myself completely and rocked backward, making us groan in tandem. We knew each other's bodies well by now, but every time we had sex felt like the first time. I'd never grow tired of tasting him, of having him inside me, of making him hard.

The broad expanse of his chest flattened my breasts. His left hand took a good grip of my bottom and wedged my pelvis against his. When his lips dipped to my ear, my body molded to his. "This is why you're here, Rourke. Because you belong with me. We belong together."

His mouth crushed mine, bruising, claiming, and relentless. When I pretended to protest, he cupped my jaw in his right hand to hold me captive. Force wasn't necessary. I'd been starving for his touch, more than I'd realized. I moaned and gave over to the strength in his arms and his male scent. At my surrender, he nipped along my lips with the edge of his teeth, sending tiny explosions of pleasure to the tips of my toes. It took all of my self-control to keep from ripping his shirt off, throwing him onto the floor, and riding him until we both came.

"Enough?" He lifted his head to pose the question.

"No, damn it." With a small sigh, I nestled my nose into the familiar notch of his collarbone. "It'll never be enough."

His wide shoulders shadowed the light from above. An earthy chuckle rumbled through his ribcage. We fit together too well. And maybe, just maybe, I enjoyed the drama of this life.

I curled my fingers into the fabric of his shirt. "Don't let go."

"Never. Not now. Not ever."

His promise rang in my ears. This man—this complicated, arrogant, stubborn man—had captured my heart, and I would never let him go.

Satan's baby baking inside you." He brandished the glass in the air between us. "You don't mind if I do then?"

"Why are you acting like this?"

"I should have known better." His bitter laughter echoed around the empty room. "Well, you won't have to worry about me anymore. I'm out of here."

"Wait. Please don't go. Let's talk about this." The dangerous glint in his eyes frightened me.

He strode toward the door. "There's nothing to talk about." He paused, his back to me. "Have a nice life, Cinderella. I hope you get your happy ending."

By the time my brain wrapped around his words, he was gone. I snapped into action and trotted after him as fast as my bare feet would allow.

Roman appeared on the landing and caught my arm. "Let him go."

"He's upset. He might do something stupid." My heart squeezed at the memory of his expression. Even though we were at odds, a part of me cared for him.

"He'll be fine. He loves himself too much to do anything harmful." Roman pulled me into his embrace. His lips brushed my hair. "If it makes you feel better, I'll check on him later. He'll probably get rip-roaring drunk, pick up a lovely girl, and break her heart before morning. Everything will go back to the way it was. You'll see."

CHAPTER 27
ROURKE

The next day, Everly arrived at the penthouse after lunch. The moment the elevator doors opened into our foyer, she ran across the living room and threw her arms around my neck. I grunted at the impact. "Thank goodness. You're okay."

"I'm fine. Except you're squashing me." I wriggled to loosen her grasp.

"Are you sure?" She relinquished her hold and held me at arm's length. Her discerning gaze scanned my body from head to toe. Finally, satisfied, her shoulders lowered. "I was so worried. I feel terrible about Daddy. You were right about him." Her voice caught. "He wants to hurt you."

"Don't worry about us. Roman and Spitz have us on lockdown. No one gets in or out of the building without their consent."

"I know. They practically strip-searched me at the door." A faint smile twisted her mouth. "That's the most action I've gotten in a while."

"How are you doing?" I drew her deeper into the living room, where we could talk. We sat on the loveseat in the corner. Despite the bright sunshine streaming through the windows and the sparkling Manhattan skyline, a sense of gloom hung over the penthouse.

"I'm going to be okay." She sounded like she was convincing herself more than me. "I told the investigators everything I knew about Lavender and Daddy, but I don't think they're going to do anything about it. He has the officials in this city in his hip pocket."

I took her hand, wishing I could ease some of her anguish. "You did a brave thing, Everly. I know it couldn't have been easy for you."

"I hope it helps." With her usual spark, she summoned an easy shrug. "I just wanted to stop by and make sure you were good before I left."

"Where are you going?" Roman sauntered into the room, barefoot and relaxed in a pair of tan drawstring pants and a soft white sweater. He paused to give me a kiss before shaking Everly's hand.

"Androvia. Prince Henry has asked me to join him over there for the summer, and I've accepted the invitation." A wall of secrecy shuttered her gaze. "The paparazzi have surrounded my house. They're following me everywhere. I need to get away."

"You're welcome to stay here," I said, glancing up at Roman for reassurance.

"Absolutely. For as long as you want." His hand wandered to my shoulder and squeezed. "But you'd be smart to get out of the country until this blows over. I'm sure your father won't be happy to hear of your friendship with Prince Henry."

The old, familiar twinkle sparked in her eyes. "Oh, I'm pretty sure he'll be livid. Especially when he hears that Henry has asked me to marry him, and I've accepted."

I blinked, certain I'd misheard her. "Wait. What?"

She nodded.

"You don't even know him."

"No, I don't." With a reassuring smile, she stood and smoothed the front of her dress. "I should get going. He's waiting for me in the car."

"Everly, no. You can't be serious." I trotted after her, leaving Roman alone in the middle of the room.

"My mind is made up. You can't change it." She pressed the elevator call button and faced me, her chin jutting stubbornly. "I've made nothing but poor choices when it comes to men. My ex-husband, then Nicky. I'm done with love. This marriage is nothing more than a business deal. I'll have everything my heart desires."

"Everything but love," I said, my chest filling with sadness. My gaze caught Roman's. He was seated in his favorite chair, reading on his tablet. His answering smile made butterflies flutter in my stomach. She had no idea what she was sacrificing.

"Love is for fairytales and the two of you." She shrugged, her nonchalance breaking my heart. "What was it Nicky always said? Not everyone gets their happily-ever-after."

"I wish you'd reconsider." The elevator dinged to announce its arrival. My mouth went dry. "Please don't go. I need you."

"No. You don't. You have Roman, and you'll have a sweet little baby to take care of soon. It's time for us to go our separate ways, Rourke." Tears pooled in the corners of my eyes. She hugged me close. "I'm happy for you. Can't you be happy for me too?"

As much as I wanted to, I couldn't say those words, not when I didn't mean them. "I'll come and visit you in Androvia. And you can come here. Promise me, Everly."

"I promise. And we can Skype." She squeezed me tighter. With a huge sigh, she stepped into the elevator. "I love you."

"I love you, too. Call me as soon as you get there."

The elevator doors closed, taking her downstairs and out of my life. My eyes burned. I choked on a sob and buried my face in my hands.

"Hey, what's wrong?" Roman, sensing my distress, had come to my side. He turned me to face him and wrapped his strong arms around me. "Please don't cry. I can't take it."

"I think I'm having a nervous breakdown," I said, swiping at the tears.

"No one's going to blame you for that." He took my chin in his fingers and tilted my face to his. "She'll be okay, Rourke. Prince Henry will take care of her."

"I hope so," I said, but I couldn't shake the feeling that our lives would never be the same.

CHAPTER 28
ROMAN

TWO MONTHS LATER...

I tapped on Rourke's office door and entered without knocking. She paced around the room, Bluetooth in her ear, and one hand on the small of her back. A high-waisted red dress swirled around the swell of her pregnant belly. Behind her, the wall of windows offered a clear view of Manhattan's skyline. She lifted a finger for me to wait, a move she'd stolen from me. I bit back a smile and ignored her request. Instead, I crossed the room, put my arms around her swollen stomach, and dragged her back to my front.

"Malcolm, we need you to sign those contracts and get them over to us right away." She rested the back of her head on my shoulder and blinked up at me. I fell headlong into the flutter of her lacy black lashes and doe eyes. "If you're having second thoughts on this partnership, our feelings won't be hurt. We have an interested party is waiting in the wings, ready to take your place."

Pride burned through my chest. She'd exceeded my expectations in every way, sharing control of the more delicate aspects of my business and proving herself as a formidable partner. I hadn't told her yet, but I planned to make her a vice president in the near future. I placed my mouth against her free ear. "Hang up."

She shook her head and frowned. The silky ends of her hair whispered over my chin. "The contracts were due yesterday. I've already give you a twenty-four hour extension. If you can't uphold your side of the deal, we're prepared to walk way." I chuckled at her show of force and was reprimanded with a scowl. She broke free from my embrace. The heels of her shoes clicked on the floor as she strode to her desk. With a few expert clicks on the keyboard, she shut down her computer and rolled her eyes. "No. No extensions. You've had more than enough time to consider the offer. If you don't comply with the deadline, we'll consider it a refusal and pursue other avenues. I'm not going to argue with you about it." She ended the call, removed the earpiece, and tossed it into her desk drawer.

"Wow. You're brutal, Mrs. Menshikov," I said, unable to hold back my wide smile.

"I learned from the best." The edge of her white teeth bit into her lower lip. "You don't think I was too harsh, do you?"

"You were perfect." The tension in her shoulders relaxed at my approval. Sunlight caught her eyes, bringing out the intense sky blue of her irises, and stirring desire deep in my gut. "Have I told you lately how much I love you?"

"Twice before breakfast and once on the drive here, but I'd like to hear it again." A radiant smile dawned across her face. My heart hammered against my ribs, the same way it had the very first time we met.

"I love you." I smoothed her hair over her shoulders. The silky strands caressed my skin and sent a shiver of desire to my dick.

"I love you too." When she returned to my embrace, I crushed her to me. She wriggled in protest, her voice filled with laughter. "You're smashing the baby."

Overwhelming emotion swelled inside me, filling all the empty spaces until I felt like bursting at the seams. Fuck me if it wasn't the greatest sensation in the world. I'd crushed rebel armies and built corporate empires, but none of those experiences topped the honor of being Rourke's husband. She buried her face in my neck. Her warm breath tickled my neck. I ran my hands up her back. Thoughts of my parents and Ivan and all the people I'd lost during my lifetime flooded my head. I clung tighter to her, wanting to keep her in my arms forever. "I'm not sure what I did to deserve you, but I'll never let you go. You need to know that."

"I'm not going anywhere, Roman." The smell of her honey and citrus body spray drifted to my nose. I drew in her scent and clung tighter to her. Somehow she understood my feelings without my saying them. "I'll never leave you."

"I know." My throat tightened, making words difficult. I held onto her, absorbing her warmth, until something prodded my stomach.

"Oh." She laughed and eased out of my grip. "The baby just kicked. Did you feel it?"

"Yes." Wonder erased my insecurities. We'd created a new life—a new Menshikov was about to inherit my kingdom.

"See. I told you not to smash him." She rubbed circles over her stomach and smiled. The previous day's sonogram had revealed the baby's sex as male. Although I loved Milada, the idea of an heir to carry on the Menshikov name fulfilled my greatest dreams.

"He's already a fighter." Visions of my son danced through my imagination. Would he be dark like me or golden like his mother? I didn't give a damn one way or the other, as long as he was healthy and happy.

"Of course he is. He's your child." A glow of contentment illuminated her creamy complexion. She slipped her hand into mine. "I'm starving. Can we go to lunch now?"

"Absolutely. The car is waiting."

We held hands on the way to the elevator. Spitz met us in the lobby and rode down with us to the parking garage. When the doors opened, our security team hustled us into the waiting Escalade. Five bodyguards accompanied us everywhere. Spitz rode in our armored vehicle. The remaining four team members followed in an identical SUV. Rourke turned to the window and sighed as we passed through the shadows of the parking garage and into the bright daylight of bustling Manhattan.

"Hey, what's the heavy sigh about?" I reached across the car to find her hand.

She threaded her fingers through mine and mustered a smile. "He's out there somewhere, isn't he? Watching us?"

Although she never mentioned his name, I knew exactly who she was talking about. Mr. McElroy had managed to escape indictment for Lavender's murder. Although he'd retreated from the public eye and the ensuing scandal, his minions continued to shadow our movements. I squeezed her hand. "You don't have to worry about him."

Spitz leaned out from the front seat. "We have twenty-four-seven surveillance on him, Mrs. Menshikov." The tension between my wife and chief of security had dissipated over the past couple of months and evolved into grudging respect. He gave her a confident smile. "That bastard can't take a shit without one of our men knowing about it."

"That's comforting." She rolled her eyes but smiled.

"He'll never get to us. You have my word." I pulled her hand to my lips and kissed her knuckles. She bit her lower lip, a telltale sign of her worry. I wanted to tell her Don McElroy's days on Earth were numbered. One of these days, he'd let his guard down, and my men would be there to exact revenge. I wanted to tell her, but I didn't. I could tell by the look in her eyes, she already knew.

When the driver turned the Escalade onto the tarmac at the airport, she lifted her eyebrows. "What's going on?"

"I have a surprise planned for you." I kept my voice nonchalant, but inside, adrenalin raced through my veins.

"A trip?" The sparkle in her eyes sent my heart over the moon. She wrenched her fingers from my grasp and pressed a palm to her chest.

"We never had a honeymoon. I thought we should take one now before the baby comes."

"Roman, no. We can't." With each word, her voice climbed higher. "I'm in the middle of contract negotiations with Malcolm. I don't have any clothes." The golden waves of her hair rippled as she shook her head. "You're crazy."

"I'm perfectly sane. You've been working too hard, and you're going to take a break. I insist." When she opened her mouth to make an excuse, I pressed a fingertip to her soft lips. "I've already spoken with your doctor, and you're cleared to fly. Your bags are packed and on the plane."

Her mouth bowed into a smile. "You've thought of everything, haven't you?"

"Damn straight I have." I unbuckled my seat belt and slid to her side. Taking her chin between my thumb and index finger, I tilted her face up to mine. "If there's anything I've forgotten, let me know. I'll go to the ends of the earth to make you happy. I'd give you the moon, if you asked for it."

"I don't need anything but you." The tip of her tongue slid over her bottom lip. With a sigh, she closed her eyes and leaned in for a kiss. Our mouths met, and the world screeched to a halt. If I lived to be a hundred years old, I'd never stop loving her.

ROURKE

I awoke to the sound of crashing waves and wind. After a healthy stretch, I sat up in bed and blinked. Above the canopy of the bed, dark wood beams crossed the ceiling. Gauzy white curtains fluttered on a sea breeze. The wall in front of me had been folded aside to reveal a panoramic, open air view of the ocean and beach. After the drab concrete and steel of Manhattan, the vibrant turquoise of the water and the brilliant explosion of flowers along the pathway to the beach seemed unreal. I drew in a lungful of salt air and blinked back tears of amazement.

After a six hour flight, a helicopter ride, and a short boat trip, we'd arrived on a tiny island in the Caribbean. Roman's *private* island. Being the wife of a billionaire definitely had its perks. I swept a hand over his side of the bed, missing him. The sheets felt cool to the touch. I had no idea how long I'd been asleep.

Movement on the beach caught my eye. Roman emerged from the surf, naked and sun-bronzed. Droplets of water glistened on his hard body, caught in the wiry hairs of his chest and the happy trail leading to his groin. He shook his head, flinging the wetness from his black hair. My heart skipped a beat. No man had ever been more perfect, from his broad shoulders down to his muscular thighs and perfect cock. *My husband.* A thrill raced through me. I resisted the urge to pinch myself. This was my life. My life. Mine. How had I gotten so lucky?

"You're up." He picked up a thick beach towel from the chaise at the edge of the patio and dragged the plush cotton over his body. His lazy grin stirred butterflies in my belly. "About time."

"How long have I been asleep?" I glanced around for a clock.

"It's noon."

"Seriously?" I threw back the covers and started to get out of bed. My stomach growled, reminding me that I hadn't eaten in forever. "I'm starving. Do we have anything to eat?" We were alone on the island. No servants. No wifi. No paparazzi. Just clear turquoise water and infinite blue skies.

He crossed the patio and entered the room, his bare feet slapping on the tile floor. "No. Stay. You need your rest, and there's no hurry." He bent to drop a kiss on the tip of my nose. I watched as he pulled on a pair of white draw-string pants. The waistband hung low enough to reveal the deep cut of muscle below each hip bone. "I made lunch for us. I was just waiting for you to wake up."

"You can cook?"

"Of course." My nipples tightened at the sight of his handsome, cocky smirk. "Have some faith, Mrs. Menshikov." After a lingering caress of my cheek, he disappeared into the hall.

I pulled on a loose-fitting sundress and paused to admire my growing baby bump. The nausea had subsided at the end of my first trimester. Aside from a ravenous appetite and dwindling stamina, I felt great. I loved having Roman's baby inside me. Each day, I marveled at the miracle of the life we were creating together. "I can't wait to meet you, little one." I rubbed the protrusion on my left side, imagining a tiny knee or elbow pressing against the wall of my womb.

Roman returned carrying a bamboo tray filled with grilled chicken, fresh pineapple and papaya, and mixed salad greens. He set the food on the patio table and came to my side. Bending down, he placed a kiss on the center of my belly. "I can't wait to meet you either."

We ate lunch in the shade of towering palm trees and

talked about names for the baby and decor for the nursery. Afterward, Roman led me down to the beach for a short tour of the grounds. The sweet fragrance of flowers surrounded us. He plucked a an orchid from one of the flower beds and tucked it behind my ear. "There. Now you look like a true island girl."

"Thank you." Despite my excitement at being in a new place, I covered my mouth to hide a yawn. "I'm sorry."

"Don't apologize. You've been working way too hard when you need to be taking it easy." He threaded his fingers through mine, his blue eyes shining with warmth. "Come on. I know just what you need."

A few yards down the sandy path, we came to a clearing. Over a patch of lush green grass, a white hammock had been tied between four sturdy trees. I eyed it warily. My past experiences with these contraptions had been less than positive. "Um, I'm not so sure about this."

"It'll be fine. Don't be a worry wart." In a graceful motion, he stretched out on his back, sinking into the soft pillows, and pulled me down beside him. "See? Perfectly stable."

"This is heavenly." With a sigh, I curled into his side and rested my cheek on his bare chest. Beneath my ear, his heart thumped in a steady, reassuring rhythm. The sound of his pulse, the gentle sway of the hammock, and the distant rush of the incoming tide lulled me into a state of extreme relaxation.

"Happy?" His deep voice rumbled through his chest. The tips of his fingers stroked along my arm.

I sighed. "Yes. Extremely." Never in my life had I experienced so much bliss. I had the man of my dreams, his baby growing inside me, and the promise of his undying love. We'd been to hell and back since our wedding. After all the drama and stress, my Prince Charming had brought me to heaven.

Under the lacy canopy of palm trees, we held each other.

Neither of us spoke. Words couldn't express my feelings in that moment. Thanks to my billionaire prince, I was the wealthiest woman in the world. Not with money or cars or power but with love and happiness and contentment. I'd found my happily ever after.

EPILOGUE

ROURKE

FOUR YEARS LATER...

A warm summer breeze blew through the willow trees surrounding the lake. Fluffy white clouds shimmered on the water's surface. I leaned back on the blanket near the shore and drew in a lungful of fresh country air. To my left, a rabbit paused to stare at me before darting into the woods behind us. To my right, my son ran across the smooth lawn, his little legs eating up the ground.

"Mommy, Mommy!" Grayson squealed in delight. No words had ever sounded more beautiful.

"Hey, there you are." I caught him in my arms and rained kisses over his face. "I missed you." He tried to squirm out of my embrace, but I squeezed him tighter. "You taste like chocolate. Did you have a good time at the store with Daddy?"

"Yes. We had ice cream." Smears of chocolate ice cream rimmed his full mouth.

"And where is Daddy?" I shielded my eyes from the sun with a hand above my eyebrows.

"There." Grayson pointed a finger toward the house.

My heart skipped a beat at the sight of my husband cresting the hill with our youngest, Claire, balanced on his shoulders. His blue eyes shone in the sunlight. Claire's chubby hands clung to her father's dark hair. The smile on his lips grew broader as our gazes collided.

"There you go." Roman hoisted Claire to the ground. She barreled into me, burying her head in my swollen belly.

"Easy now," I said, smoothing her blond curls. "Momma has a baby in her belly, remember?"

"Yes." Claire's blue eyes, shaped exactly like mine, brightened. "In there." She poked my stomach with a finger.

"That's right. You have a baby brother or sister inside Momma's tummy." Roman bent down to kiss me then rubbed my belly. "Hi, little one." He eased onto the blanket beside me, stretching his long legs in front of us. "Did you miss us?"

"Every second," I teased. "But it was nice to have a few minutes to myself. Thank you." I brushed my lips over his, feeling the same flutter of nerves I'd experienced the very first time we'd met.

Between work and the children, moments alone had been few and far between. Grayson's abundant energy and restless spirit kept me on my toes. Once Claire had been born, Roman and I had started working from home to share the responsibility. Our third child, another boy, was due next month.

"Everly called," I said, drawing Claire onto my lap. She laid her head on my chest. Her long, lacy eyelashes fanned out over her cheeks, weighed down by sleep. Within seconds, her breathing evened out. Her thumb crept into her mouth. I caressed her silky hair. Unbridled devotion consumed me. "She's coming home for her father's funeral."

Mr. McElroy's private plane had crashed in a field last week. I had to wonder if Roman had played a part in the accident. I didn't ask. Although McElroy had never been formally charged with Lavender's murder, his reputation and marriage had been irreparably damaged. A part of me mourned the man who'd been so kind to me during my childhood. The rest of me would sleep easier at night knowing he was no longer a threat.

"Is Henry coming with her?" Roman caught Grayson by the back of his pants just in time to keep him from plunging headfirst into the lake. "Whoa, son."

"I'm not sure. Probably. We didn't discuss the details." Although we talked on the phone weekly, our conversations centered around our children and current events. She sounded happy. The duties of the royal court kept her busy, and Henry seemed to adore her. I shifted Claire, not wanting to wake her but needing relief from the extra pressure on my bladder. "Can you take her? I've got to pee again."

"Of course." He eased her out of my arms then offered a hand to help me up.

I groaned and rubbed the arch of my back. I'd gained an extra twenty pounds with this baby and felt every ounce in my joints.

"Grayson, help your mommy."

"Okay." Grayson wrapped his pudgy hand around two of my fingers and tugged me up the hill toward the house.

"Wait." I stopped, feeling tears spring to my eyes.

"Is something wrong?" Roman's expression sobered, his voice rising in alarm.

"No. I just want to savor this moment before it's gone." From the crest of the hill, sunlight glinted off the windows of our sprawling mansion. Horses grazed beyond the white fences of their paddocks. I had two beautiful children at my feet, a baby on the way, and the most perfect man in the world at my side. Life had never been better. Our eyes met.

"Thank you." I choked on the words. "You've given me more than I ever dreamed possible."

He smiled at me over the top of Claire's head. "It's been my pleasure, Mrs. Menshikov." The focus of his gaze dipped to my lips. "I can think of a few ways you could show your appreciation."

"Oh, really? How's that?" Excitement stirred in my belly. I knew that look.

Grayson tugged impatiently on my fingers. "Come on, Mommy. Let's go. Let's go."

"How about a date night at The Devil's Playground?" His eyebrows lifted in wicked inquiry.

We hadn't been there in a very long time. My heart began to pound against my ribs. The playful mischief in his expression warmed my heart and sent a pulse of attraction into my core. "It's a date," I said and slipped my free hand into his.

The four of us climbed the hill together. As we walked into the setting sun, my hopes soared. Rourke Donahue was gone, and I didn't miss her. I'd been reborn as Mrs. Menshikov, wife to the exiled prince and war king. Roman's bloodline would survive for another generation, and the Menshikov dynasty had risen from the ashes of destruction to rule once again.

🙰🙰🙰

THANK YOU FOR READING *THE WAR KING*. I HOPE YOU'LL enjoy this preview of the standalone novel, *The Rebel Queen*.

🙰🙰🙰

"DON'T LOOK AT HIM. HE'S NOT IN CHARGE HERE. YOU answer to me and only me." Even though Henry's tone echoed with authority, his eyes teased me playfully.

"I answer to no one but myself," I replied.

His fingers wrapped around my upper arm. He half-dragged, half-walked me into the chamber adjoining the throne room. "You can't defy me in public—in front of my staff, Everly. I'm the king. How are people going to respect me when you're constantly defiant?"

He took a step closer, shrinking the gap between us in one stride. Instinctively, I took a step back. He followed me until my backside hit the cool paneling. He braced one hand against the wood beside my head, trapping me. The scent of his aftershave brought back distant memories of campfires and rain. By the look of his bare jaws, he'd just shaved.

Unable to stop myself, I stroked a hand down the smooth curve of his cheek and stopped at the dimple in his chin. What would it be like to kiss those full lips? To feel the slide of his tongue against mine? My knees melted at the thought.

"You know, in the days of my grandfather, I could have had you beheaded for that kind of insubordination to your king." He leaned closer, bringing with him the fresh scent of his cologne and shower gel.

"You're not my king," I said.

"Not yet, anyway." The sheer amount of cockiness in his reply sparked my rebellious nature. His piercing gaze took in every plane and plateau on my face before coming to a stop at my eyes. His breath puffed against my lips. It smelled of peppermint and sugar. "But that's about to change. Soon."

"Do you hear yourself?" A bubble of laughter swelled in my chest. It burst, sending the sound into the room. Henry frowned. I placed a hand on my stomach and tried to steady myself. "Oh my goodness. Are you seriously that arrogant?"

"I think you're confusing arrogance with confidence. I know who I am and what I want. Can you say the same?"

His question hit me hard. Who was I? The unruly daughter of a disgraced Vice President? The former director of a non-profit organization? A socialite? I sifted through the many titles I'd worn, titles given to me by other people, and came up empty-handed. "Why do you have to be such an ass?" I asked, lifting my chin in defiance.

"You knew I was an ass when you married me. Don't let your daddy issues get the better of you."

His observation raised my temper another notch. "I can't believe you said that." The first part was true. I couldn't fault him for it. I'd married him willingly to escape the social media shit storm around my father and the baggage of my past. But the second part? He couldn't have been more wrong. "You don't know anything about me." Even though I'd vowed to remain numb to his insults and goading, tears stung the backs of my eyelids.

He took a step backward, his expression shifting into neutral. His jaw, impossibly square and so damn strong, tensed. After an exhausted sigh, he ran his hands through his hair. When he spoke, his voice was soft and low. "No. I don't, but I'm willing to change that." I leaned closer to catch his words. His lips nuzzled my ear. "I apologize."

Two little words had never meant so much to me. Their unexpectedness stole my voice. I cleared my throat. "I'm sorry. What was that?" I'd never heard him apologize to anyone for anything—ever. And although I'd heard him loud and clear, I couldn't resist the opportunity to goad him.

His gray-green gaze watched me from beneath hooded lids. One corner of his mouth twitched. "You know bloody damn well what I said."

Sexual tension crackled in the air between us. He rolled his head on his neck and stood up straighter. The fabric of his sweater stretched across his hard chest. He stared at me down the length of his nose, looking every bit the king.

Following his lead, I whispered in his ear, "Say it again."

He snorted, breaking into a full smile. "You heard me the

first time." My skin heated from the warmth of it. "Do I sound like I'm a contender for the Iron Throne?" Sunlight caught the highlights in his blond hair as he shook his head. "Sometimes I'm an ass."

"Sometimes?" I lifted an eyebrow.

"Fine. All the time."

I covered my mouth in mock surprise. "Wow. We actually agree on something."

"Yes. At least we've got that going for us." He ran a hand down the length of my arm. His fingers slid through mine, sending tingles of desire into my center. "You *will* bend the knee to me, Your Majesty." That adorable grin, the one that filled me with frustration and made my pussy pulse with need, twitched his lips.

"I won't."

He shook his head, amused by my refusal. "Oh, you will. I promise you."

৩়৯৫

I hope you enjoyed this preview of *The Rebel Queen*. Now available for pre-order.

৩়৯৫

Need more? Check out this LIMITED TIME OFFER!

Over 20 illicit romances with the sexy heroes and strong heroines you crave!

Lose yourself in the world of hot hookups, where the stories run from sexy to downright scandalous and the

JEANA E. MANN

characters will leave you breathless. In these pages, you'll find tantalizing romance, rekindled flames, and forbidden trysts.

FROM CONFIDENT MILITARY MEN AND SUAVE BILLIONAIRES to bad boy players, hot alphas, and more, you're sure to find the illicit romance of your fantasies burning up these pages! These powerful, exciting men will keep you up all night and daydreaming all day!

YOUR FAVORITE CONTEMPORARY ROMANCE AUTHORS INVITE you to join them for over twenty sizzling stories. Which of these scorching novels and novellas will have you hooked?

DON'T DELAY YOUR PLEASURE. ONE-CLICK TODAY!

ALSO BY JEANA E. MANN

Felony Romance Series

Intoxicated

Unexpected

Vindicated

Impulsive

Drift

Committed

Pretty Broken Series

Pretty Broken Girl

Pretty Filthy Lies

Pretty Dirty Secrets

Pretty Wild Thing

Pretty Broken Promises

Pretty Broken Dreams

Pretty Broken Baby

Pretty Broken Hearts

Pretty Broken Bastard

Standalones

Monster Love

Short Stories

Everything

Linger

The Exiled Prince Trilogy

STAY IN TOUCH

Never miss a new release.

Subscribe to Jeana's newsletter and get the inside scoop on new and upcoming releases, marketing information, FREE BOOKS, sales, book signings, giveaways, and much more!

CLICK HERE

You may unsubscribe at any time. Your information will never be shared without your express permission.

TEXT ALERTS

Text the word "Jeana" (without quotation marks) to 21000 and receive new release alerts straight to your phone.

BEFORE YOU GO

DID YOU ENJOY READING THIS BOOK?
If you did, please help others enjoy it, too.

- **Lend it.**
- **Recommend it.**
- **Review it.**

HELP AN AUTHOR — LEAVE A REVIEW:
If you leave a *positive* review, please send me an email at jeanamann@yahoo.com or a message on Facebook so that I can thank you with a personal email.

ABOUT THE AUTHOR

Jeana Mann is the author of sizzling hot contemporary romance. Her debut release *Intoxicated* was a First Place Winner of the 2013 Cleveland Rocks Romance Contest, a finalist in the Carolyn Readers' Choice Awards, and fourth place winner in the International Digital Awards. She is a member of Romance Writers' of America (RWA).

Jeana was born and raised in Indiana where she lives today with her two crazy rat terriers Mildred and Mabel. She graduated from Indiana University with a degree in Speech and Hearing, something totally unrelated to writing. When she's not busy dreaming up steamy romance novels, she loves to travel anywhere and everywhere. Over the years she climbed the ruins of Chichen Iza in Mexico, snorkeled along the shores of Hawaii, driven the track at the Indy 500, sailed around Jamaica, ate gelato on the steps of the Pantheon in Rome, and explored the ancient city of Pompeii. More important than the places she's been are the people she has met along the way.

Be sure to connect with Jeana on Facebook or follow along on Twitter for the latest news regarding her upcoming releases.

Connect with Jeana at
www.jeanaemann.net
jeanamann@yahoo.com

TEXT ALERTS -
Text the word "Jeana" without quotation marks to 21000 and
get all the latest marketing news plus new release alerts
straight to your phone.

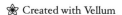